a holly, holly christmas

Mikal Dawn

121
PUBLISHING HOUSE
I lift my eyes to the mountains...

Cover photos:
Front cover design by: Mikal Hermanns
Indian Bride: DeborahKolb/depositphotos.com
Scottish Groom: dasha11/depositphotos.com
Ice Castle: rusty426/depositphotos.com

First edition, 121 Publishing House, 2020

For Jesus. Always first. This is all because of You.

Mark, I love you. Thank you for being my #1.

Lyndsey, I adore you! Thank you for your prayers and encouragement. You're a true gift, my friend.

January

CHAHNA: I MET SOMEONE!

LEILAH: YOU MEAN YOUR PARENTS SET YOU UP WITH SOMEONE?

CHAHNA: HA!

CATE: HOW DID YOU MEET HIM THEN? TELL ME MOORRREEE!!

LYDIA: DETAILS, PLEASE.

CATE: TELL ME MOOOOOORRRRREEEE.

HANADY: SERIOUSLY, SPILL ALREADY!

CHAHNA: WELL, HE'S A POLICE OFFICER, SCOTTISH, RED HAIR...

CATE: HELLO. PIC? AND HOW DID YOU MEET?

CHAHNA: HE TAGGED ME FOR JAYWALKING. NO SHAME! ESPECIALLY SINCE I MET HIM.

LEILAH: JAYWALKING? IS THAT EVEN A THING POLICE TICKET PEOPLE FOR? LOL! BUT WHAT ABOUT YOUR PARENTS? ARE THEY STILL TRYING TO SET YOU UP?

CHAHNA: HE TOLD ME HE ONLY STOPPED ME SO HE COULD MEET ME. I MELTED. HIS PARTNER WAS CRACKING UP. AND OF COURSE MY PARENTS ARE STILL TRYING TO SET ME UP. BUT IF THIS THING WITH MAGUIRE GOES SOMEWHERE, THEN IT SHOULD TAKE CARE OF THAT.

CATE: MAGUIRE? IS THAT HIS LAST NAME?

CHAHNA: NOPE, MAGUIRE WILSON. HE TOLD ME I CAN CALL HIM MAG.

CHAHNA: AND I JUST GOT BUTTERFLIES. I HAVE BUTTERFLIES!

chapter one

Early October

er watch buzzed her wrist with an incoming call. Sliding her finger across the watch face, Chahna Kapoor answered just as the Powell/Hyde route cable car clanged its bell rumbling up Jones Street, as if it were racing her. Fat chance she'd win. She didn't have cables and a motor to push her body up the hill.

"Chahna Kapoor with J. Dawson Designs. How may I help you?" Hopefully the caller could make out her words over her huffing and puffing. She really needed to work out more.

"I'm sorry, I didn't hear your name, and I don't want to pronounce it incorrectly." The accent surprised her.

"Oh, sorry! It's pronounced just like Shawna."

"What a belle name."

Ah. French. But not quite French. Her curiosity was killing her almost as much as the tourists hanging out the back of the cable car trying to catch one last glimpse of the bay and Yerba Buena Island before turning the corner.

"Thank you," she smiled—she'd heard once that if you smile when you talk, it comes through the phone lines and puts the listener at ease. "How may I help you?"

"Ah, yes. I'm Noémie from Hôtel de Glace."

Oh no. She was having a heart attack, she was sure of it. Ana dropped her bag to the ground and pressed her hand over her heart. Oh good. Still beating. She drew a deep breath.

"I'm calling about your inquiry from a year ago."

Talk about customer service. When she'd submitted her request online, they'd responded almost immediately letting her know they were booked over two years in advance. At that point, she hadn't been dating anyone, but she just knew she was close. Too bad she hadn't been as close as she thought. But now with Mag...

"We've had a cancellation and were wondering if you would like this date?"

"Wow!" She stretched out her left hand and eyed the empty spot where the ring would go. "I'd be happy to accept, thank you." Surely, he would propose soon, right?

"Oh, uh...wouldn't you like to know the date first?"

Chahna waved a hand in front of her face. Semantics. "Of course," she giggled. She and Mag had only been dating around ten months, but she knew he was the one.

Her parents, on the other hand... She let that thought slide. They were just being dramatic—par for the course when one had Bollywood stars for parents. And they were romantics at heart, constantly trying to set her up, no matter that Mag was in the picture. They probably couldn't imagine that she and Mag were as committed as they truly were since they'd never been able to clear their filming schedules to fly out from Mumbai to meet him. Hopefully once they met Mag, they'd calm down.

"Great, then I'll put your name down for December 23rd. We are so very happy for you and your fiancé. I will email you a confirmation along with a form to collect some other information."

"Thank you, Noémie."

Wait. December 23rd of what year? Since they typically booked a year or two out, it had to be next year, right? So, she had that long to get engaged and plan her wedding? And let Maguire know of the venue. She grimaced. Her beach-loving Scot really wasn't a fan of winter. But she had a year to talk him into it. And get her parents to visit so they could meet him.

"Thank you, Chahna. Au revoire!"

Ana tapped her phone and ended the call. A text had come in while she was talking. Oh! Her tribe. She loved her college friends, Hanady, Lydia,

Cate, Ruth Ann, and Leilah. Cate had been her roommate and became her best friend. The other girls lived in the same house and were close friends, too. She missed them all since they were spread out from coast to coast. As if to remind her where she lived, another trolley dinged its bell and rumbled by. She must have been standing outside her office building for a while. Thankfully, despite the time of year, it was still mild weather. October in San Francisco often hovered around 70-degrees. She could handle that.

She hearted the selfie Hanady had sent of her and Keenan and entered the building in front of her. Did the running shoes she wore to walk to work squeak on the marble floor as she skipped through the doors? Maybe. Did she have a wide grin glued to her face? Most definitely. Did the two other people waiting for the lift look at her as if she were insane? Of course. Did she care? Not whatsoever. She only wished she had a hat she could twirl and throw in the air like that character, Mary Richards, in that old TV show.

She had her dream wedding venue.

"Wilson!"

Maguire turned, a hand running over his chin where he preferred a beard to be. "Hey, Lin. Is my favorite partner back on duty?"

"Yeah, but wishing I could take more time off."

Mag slapped Jason on the back. "Ten days isn't enough, is it? But we chose the blue life, right?"

Lin shook his head. "No, the blue life chose us." His partner grinned, a sigh escaping where a normal person would have chuckled. But his friend didn't chuckle like normal people. He sighed.

"How's Maya?"

Jason's wide grin shrunk and he raked his fingers through his jet-black hair. "I really hope it takes this time. Maya's still broken up over the last time. Don't get me wrong, I am too." He grimaced then added, "So's the bank account."

He'd never asked, but knew Jason and Maya lived well below their already not high means. Police officers made good money in San Francisco...if they lived in Wyoming. Living in the city, however, was expensive. And that was putting it mildly. Add in vitro fertilization to the already high-cost living, and Mag couldn't imagine the financial toll it was taking.

"Speaking of the bank account, are you and Ana free in two weeks? We're downsizing to save on rent and could use your help moving."

Mag didn't know how much further Jason and Maya could downsize—he'd been to their current place and while it was bigger than his own 450 square foot apartment, it just barely fit two people.

"Two weeks?" Maguire pulled out his phone and tapped on the calendar. "It looks free for me. I'll check with Ana."

"Thanks. By the way, how are things with her going? Will I be hearing wedding bells any time soon?"

The curse of being a red-headed Scot was the blush factor. The slightest embarrassment caused him to turn red as a cherry. Leave it to his partner, who knew and delighted in this fact, to embarrass him whenever he could.

He shrugged. "Maybe."

"Whoa. A couple of weeks ago, it was a 'Too soon, man.' Now we're at 'maybe'? Making progress, I see."

"Maybe you and Maya have convinced me." Mag cut his gaze to Jason. It was impossible to hold back the grin. Seeing his partner and his wife whenever they had a meal together made him imagine his own future. And Chahna Kapoor was in every single image he ever pictured.

Lin lifted his chin and studied Mag before he spoke. "You have a ring," he shoved a finger into Mag's chest.

Mag knew some partners developed a special bond, but it was a little freaky when his own partner was able to tell things like that.

"I don't." And he didn't. He'd just been looking.

Jason lifted his gaze to the ceiling of the station. "Have you met her parents yet?"

Her parents. There was an obstacle if he ever pictured one. Ana's parents were always busy filming in India, a side effect of being famous Bollywood actors. Not to mention their penchant for trying to set her up, despite him being firmly in the picture.

"Not yet, no."

"But they know about you?"

"I think they choose to forget about me."

"Because you're white?"

He laughed. "No, because I'm not their choice. I don't think me being white has any effect."

"That's a start, at least."

It was. But how was he going to get in their good books when they hadn't visited once since he and Ana had started dating? FaceTime wasn't really a replacement for actually spending time with them, and there was no way he wanted to ask her father's permission to marry her over a video call.

"Lin, Wilson!" Their sergeant's voice bellowed down the hall from the briefing room. "Think you could grace us with your presence for roll call?"

"Off to a great start of shift, aren't we?" Lin clucked his tongue and made his way down the hall, Maguire following him.

chapter two

*a*na! What in the world made you do that?" Cate's laugh resonated through the video chat.

Ana stared at the email on the shared screen she'd received from Hôtel de Glace. "I don't know," she wailed. "How do I get myself into these situations?"

The laughter continued. Ana squinted, staring at the screen. Were those tears streaking down her best friend's face?

"I think you know." Cate's grin filled the screen. "Seriously, how did you even come up with this idea?"

Chahna shoved her hands through her hair and rested her elbows on the kitchen counter. "When we were making plans for Hanady's wedding, I was Googling fun wedding venues and the Hôtel de Glace came up. Cate. It was all made of ice. The rooms were solid ice and had different themes. You should see the carvings artists do on the walls. They have a different theme each year. And the chapel!" She sighed. "The chapel was small, intimate, and oh-so perfect. There were even photos of tall ice blocks with beautiful flowers frozen inside. It was magical! I couldn't help myself, Cate," she wailed. "When the woman called this morning, I really thought she was talking December 23rd of next year. Like, fourteen months from now. Not two months from now. What do I do? Mag hasn't proposed—he hasn't even hinted at proposing. But I don't want to lose this."

"If he hasn't proposed, he hasn't proposed. It's not like you can make him do it."

Ana's head shot up and she stared at Cate. Make him do it? Could I? Her pulse throbbed. Maybe not hold a gun to his head and force him, but could she somehow set up every date as an opportunity for him to propose?

"Ana, I know that look. What are you thinking?"

"Nothing..." her voice trailed in a playful singsong.

"Ana. Don't think that British accent can get you out of it. Tell me."

Was it wrong to pretend she didn't hear her best friend? Well, even if so, too bad.

"I think we have a bad connection, Cate. I apologize. Must run! Ta ta!"

"Chahna Kapoor, don't you da—"

She clicked out of FaceTime with a quick prayer Cate would forgive her. Oh, who was she kidding? Of course she'd forgive her. Cate was sweet and full of Southern charm. It was in her nature to forgive.

Ana filled out the paperwork for the reservation, entering hers and Mag's information. She really, really hoped and prayed he'd propose soon. And would be okay with a short engagement. A very short engagement.

On the coffee table beside her MacBook, her phone buzzed. Another video chat, this time from her parents. Ana took a deep breath, held it for a moment, and slowly let it out. Another deep breath and she picked up her phone, let the breath out through her nose, and slid her thumb along the screen to answer.

"Hi Mum, hi Papa. How are you?"

"I'm dying, Chahna."

Leave it to her mother to start a call with dramatic flair. Mum believed it her right as a famous Bollywood actress. Thankfully, her father wasn't quite as dramatic though he was as famous an actor as her mother.

"I see the future of our family fading away, my daughter."

Never mind. Apparently her mother was giving her father acting lessons. And this opening gave her a hint as to where the conversation was going.

"Papa, you know I'm dating someone."

"Dating does not equal a ring on your finger." Her mother clapped her hands together and lifted her gaze upward. Praying for her daughter? Likely.

"Mum, please. We're as good as engaged." She hoped her parents didn't see her crossed fingers in her lap. "I'm sure it will happen any day now."

"That is not good enough. Besides, I was speaking with my director this morning—" Ana slumped, doing her best to keep her eyes focused on the screen, not rolling to the heavens. "He has a cousin who lives in Los Angeles with a son who lives in Sacramento. That cannot be too far, can it?" Her father waved a hand in front of his face. "Of course not. The United States is not that big."

"Papa, it's three times the size of India."

"Hmph. We shall see about that."

There was never any use in arguing with her parents, so she let that one slide.

Wait.

We will see about that? Did that mean... "Does this mean you're coming here for a visit?" They hadn't visited her since university, and with her work schedule, it was difficult for her to travel to India, despite her parents' willingness to pay for the trip and cover her expenses back home while she wasn't working. In their minds, when one visited India, one must stay at least a month. Ana's employer didn't see it that way, however, and had told her if she went, she wouldn't have a job when she came back. It was of no consequence to her parents to pay for her apartment, food, and bills in San Francisco as long as she came for a one-month (at least) visit, but there was no way she wanted to be dependent on her parents. She was a twenty-something, independent woman, not a child who needed her mummy and daddy's money.

"Yes, darling!" Her mother bounced in her seat. "Your Papa and I will be there in two days."

"Two days?!" Ana's mouth dried up.

"Yes," her father beamed. "Surprise!"

Oh, it was a surprise all right.

14

"Where will you be staying?" There was no way she had the space for them. She barely had the space for herself.

"The Fairmont Heritage Place."

The luxurious hotel was beautiful, but she suspected they stayed there more because it was one of the most, if not the most, expensive hotels in San Francisco. Plus, the location—Ghirardelli Square—was a bonus.

"That sounds amazing."

Papa nodded. "We will call you when we arrive at the hotel. You will come meet us for dinner."

"Are you sure? That's a long trip from Mumbai."

"You are our daughter. We want to see you as soon as possible."

"Okay. I'll bring Maguire with me. He's anxious to meet you."

Her parents side-eyed each other. That couldn't be a good thing. But her father leaned toward the camera and smiled—his on-screen smile. Uh oh. "Of course. Bring him."

They spoke for another minute before ending the call. Her parents were definitely characters. She loved them dearly, but their filming schedules as she was growing up necessitated boarding school. They sent her to the UK for that—hence the accent her friends, especially Leilah, adored—but it kept her from having a very close relationship with them. When she decided to go to university in the United States, and ultimately stay here, they balked. They'd hoped she would return to India and if not become a Bollywood actress herself, at least manage their careers for them. Her degree in interior design should have warned them that wouldn't be the case, but her parents lived in their own world.

A smile tugged at the corners of her mouth. Despite their differences, she adored them.

Ana stood and stretched her arms above her head before glancing at her watch. Nine o'clock. Mag would still be on shift. Maybe she could text a friend for a late dinner.

Orphan Andy's on 17th Street was one of Ana's favorite diners. It was full of food that wasn't the healthiest, but oh, was it ever comforting. And with it being open 24/7, the place was an easy choice for late dinner meetups with friends.

Chahna pulled the door open and was hit with a blast of tantalizing smells. She picked up on her favorite dish there. The rich aroma of their Hawaiian burger—her mouth watered at the thought of the pineapple and cream cheese that sounded oh-so-wrong but was oh-so-good—hit her as she spotted her friend, Carrie, and made her way past the bar to a booth near the back of the restaurant.

"Hi," Carrie stood from the table and leaned forward to wrap Ana in a quick hug.

"Hi! Thank you for saving my stomach from my cooking."

Carrie's chuckle scrunched her button nose. "I've already ordered your burger for you."

"You're a saint." She'd first met her friend online when she joined a Facebook group for newcomers to San Francisco. The two had hit it off, and when Ana arrived in her new city, they'd met up at Orphan Andy's to finally meet in person. She was always dazzled by Carrie's easy smile and warm brown eyes.

As Ana sat, she reached over to the wall and made the attached personal Jukebox sing, then sat back. "How are you?"

Carrie ran her finger along the edge of her glass of water. "I'm good." She glanced up and grinned. "Dating someone."

"What? Who, when, where, how did you meet? Tell me all!"

Her friend's shoulder-length brown curls bobbed as she bounced in her seat and spilled the details. They gabbed while they ate for over an hour before the door opened and the breeze from the bay blew in. When Carrie looked up, the size of her grin caused Ana to turn around to see for herself who walked in. And lo and behold, her favorite police offer.

"Mag!"

Maguire Wilson was everything she never knew she wanted. She usually went for tall, dark, and handsome, but Mag was tall, gingered, and—dare she say it?—hot. Her boyfriend glanced around the restaurant before he leaned over her and laid a quick kiss on her forehead. Kissing while in uniform was a no-no, but she loved those sweet, tender, and stolen kisses just as much as when he wasn't in uniform and kissed her properly.

"Hey, Lass. I didn't expect to see you here." His slight Scottish brogue from spending his youth in his homeland made her stomach do flips.

"I was starved, and didn't want to choke down my own cooking, so..." she grinned. "Are you on a break already?"

"Only for a minute. We," he jabbed his thumb over his shoulder, pointing to his partner, "came in to grab Lin's wife the Bailey's Irish Cream Cheesecake."

Jason Lin stuck his head around Mag's shoulder and threw his hand up in a wave. "Hey Ana."

She waved her fingers. "Hi Jason. How's Maya?"

The sparkle in Lin's eyes disappeared, despite the smile on his face staying in place. "She's okay."

"Give her a hug for me?"

"You bet."

Ana scooched over so Mag could sit on the edge of the booth while he waited for Jason to get his order.

"How's work going?"

"It's a quiet night." He grabbed one of Ana's leftover fries and ate it in one bite. "I'm not complaining, though."

Carrie asked Mag a question—or two, Ana wasn't really listening. How could she get Mag to propose? She knew he was the one. Had absolutely no doubts whatsoever. She couldn't imagine spending the rest of her life with anyone else. But while she was an independent woman, she didn't want to be the one to propose.

She leaned her head on his shoulder while he was talking. She didn't think he even noticed that his left hand grabbed her right, his thumb stroking the back of her hand. Everything was just so natural for them. So right.

She lifted her head and viewed his profile. His five o'clock shadow was coming in, though only visible up close and personal. The corner of his mouth lifted, like he was aware she was watching him.

Mag always seemed to know when Ana was watching him, even if she wasn't in his view. On their first date, she'd watched as he left their table to go to the men's room. Halfway there, he slowed, and as he turned, she saw the corner of his lips slide up. Then he made eye contact and winked. She was almost put off, thinking he was cocky, but his smile softened and he mouthed Be right back. She'd texted her parents about her date while she waited for him, and—

Her parents! She'd almost let that slip her mind. Ana waited for a pause in the conversation before jumping in. "Mag, I almost forgot."

His hazel gaze landed on her and she almost melted into a puddle under the table.

"Ana? Forgot what?"

Right. She gave herself a mental shake. "My parents are flying in and would like to meet for dinner Thursday night. Is that okay?"

Mag's Adam's apple bobbed before he nodded. "That sounds great."

"Really?"

He touched his forehead to hers. "Really. I'm excited to meet them."

She absolutely loved him and was ready to make him hers forever.

chapter three

*A*na bounced on her heels at baggage claim. Her parents' plane landed fifteen minutes ago, so she was sure it'd be a while before she saw them due to customs. But they were in San Francisco. To see her. And meet Mag.

She wished her boyfriend—hopefully soon-to-be fiancé—could have joined her, but it was his day off and he had an appointment he couldn't cancel. Her parents wouldn't give his absence a thought, though, since they were supposed to take a car to their hotel. She didn't decide to surprise them until that morning.

The noise level inside the airport grew as passengers started showing up and the baggage began moving onto the belts.

Ana slurped the last of the Starbucks secret menu peanut butter chocolate Frappuccino. There was nothing like a good, liquid Reese's Peanut Butter Cup to ease the nerves.

Chucking the cup into the garbage, she paced back and forth across the way from baggage claim. After circling the area several times—a girl had to get her steps in for the day, after all—she heard a woman speak in Hindi. She studied the people gathering around the claim until she spotted first her father, then her mum.

Papa had always been handsome to her. When she was little, he'd been Bollywood's heartthrob. Every woman had been jealous of Mum, though plenty of fans were jealous of Papa, too. Mum was absolutely stunning with her dark hair that was longer than most California girl's shorts and still had no grey, and her wrinkle-free skin. She really hoped she'd inherited her mother's genes.

She drew closer to her parents when she saw Mum talking to someone. A younger someone. A younger, male someone. They were standing very close together, as a matter of fact. Her father stood by them with a half-grin on his face.

Who was that guy? He seemed familiar, but she was sure she'd never met him.

As she moved closer, he half-turned and she stopped dead in her tracks.

They wouldn't have. Her hands curled into fists at her side.

Her father clapped his hand against the man's back. Her stomach clenched.

They would.

It took everything she had within her, but Ana held back a scream that likely would have sounded like a banshee. They knew she was dating Maguire. And yet they still brought the actor who'd been the hero in their last movie—their movie son.

Apparently, they were trying to make him their real-life son.

Uuuugggghhhh.

Maybe she could slip out of the airport before they saw her.

"Chahna!"

Or maybe not.

Double ugh.

Ana plastered a Hindi Barbie smile on her face—she'd picked up the acting genes, too—and waved at her parents. "Surprise." Was her smile as weak as the voice that just came out of her mouth?

Though they didn't seem as surprised by her arrival as she was by their "guest."

Papa's eyes rounded. "What are you doing here?"

Funny, she wanted to ask the stray they'd brought along the same question. Her mother at least had the grace to look slightly abashed as she glanced at the man next to her.

"I thought I'd surprise you rather than waiting until dinner tonight." She eyed the younger man. "But turns out I'm the one who's surprised."

"Chahna, hello. I'm Raj Bhatt." He flashed the brightest white smile she'd ever seen.

Well, maybe Ross's teeth in that *Friends* episode were brighter. But not by much.

Her papa wrapped his arms around her. "Hi, Love. I've missed you." He lowered his voice. "And I'm sorry. I couldn't talk her out of it."

At least he'd tried. She relaxed a little in his hug.

He leaned back and eyed her. "But is this really a bad thing?"

Guess he hadn't tried too hard. Was it still disrespectful to roll one's eyes at one's parents?

"Papa, I have a boyfriend!" And hopefully a fiancé before long.

Hm. Maybe if she told her parents she was engaged to Mag, they'd back off?

Ugh. No. He was meeting them tonight, and if they thought he'd proposed, especially without her father's consent, he'd be burned at the stake and she'd be in the doghouse.

"Chahna, are you off in your own world again?" Her mum snapped her fingers in front of her face.

Ana startled but shook her head. "No, Mum."

Her mother lifted one eyebrow. Sheesh, she hated it when her mum did that.

"It's true!"

"Mm-hm. Well," Mum looked at the luggage traveling the belt behind her. "Looks like Raj and your papa got all the bags, so we can run off. We hired a car. Since you're here, I take it you'll join us?"

When she said "us," her hand waved in the direction of Raj. Of course, she'd insinuate him. Looked like Ana wasn't going to get out of this tangled web before dinner tonight. She'd really need to find a private moment to at the very least text Mag and warn him what was going on.

"Yes. I took public transit here with hopes I could join you in your car."

21

"Then let's be off."

Ana followed her parents out of the airport and to their hired car. Too bad Raj tagged along beside her.

"Are you sure you don't want to look at the more traditional diamond rings?"

Mag glanced up from the sparkling rings encased in glass at the woman who had the most dubious smile spread across her face. "I'm sure. My girlfriend isn't ordinary diamond quality."

"Ordinary?" she sputtered. "Diamonds are far from ordinary."

"Then why does practically every married woman wear one?"

Her mouth worked like a fish. Ha! Gotcha. He supposed he should take pity on her. "But she genuinely loves aquamarines, so I'd like to go with that."

The woman shook her head, as if she didn't believe him. He could swear he heard her mutter under her breath as she turned her back and walked to another case. Sounded like, "It's your funeral." He smirked—he couldn't help it—but he knew Ana and she'd love to be different than everyone else, especially with a few of her friends getting married recently.

His pulse raced. Married. He was really thinking of doing this. They hadn't even talked about marriage. Well...that wasn't entirely true. When they watched a movie a few weeks ago and there was a wedding in it, she'd oohed and awed over it and said she couldn't wait until her own wedding day.

Little did she know he'd already been praying about asking her. It did seem like she was dropping more and more hints, especially the past few days. Walking past a bridal shop the other night, she'd stopped in her tracks and declared she was in love. She stood staring at the dress, then glanced at him. "With you. Of course. I mean, the dress is beautiful, too, and I'd love to wear—uh...so where are we going for dinner?" She wasn't as quick as she thought covering her tracks on that one.

Brittany, the salesperson helping him, moved her hand like Vanna White across the case. "Is this what you had in mind?" He was sure she was inwardly turning her nose up at his choice, but he didn't care.

"Yes. Thank you."

He studied the rings below the glass. What had Ana's best friend, Cate, told him? Something about roses... "Is there roses gold?" It sounded wrong, what could he do? He needed to get this ring right.

Brittany pulled her lips between her teeth and bit down before she released them and spoke. Was she laughing at him? Oh well. He could swallow his pride for Ana. "I believe you're looking for rose gold. And yes." She stepped to the side and stood behind another case. "Here is our collection of rose gold. I do admit that aquamarines and rose gold look quite pretty together."

Maguire's gaze was drawn immediately to one particular ring. That's it. He tapped his finger on the glass. "This one."

Brittany couldn't quite hide her surprise fast enough. He saw it and grinned. "Surprised I have good taste?"

"My lips are sealed."

He laughed. "Fair enough. Is it possible to take it out and get a better look? Maybe send a picture to my girlfriend's friend to get her final approval?"

"Of course, sir."

It didn't take long for Cate to reply with one word, all caps.

CATE: YES!!!!!

MAGUIRE: IT ISN'T TOO MUCH?

CATE: ARE YOU KIDDING ME?! OF COURSE NOT!

MAGUIRE: THANKS CATE.

CATE: I'M DYING. WHEN ARE YOU PLANNING ON DOING THIS?

He didn't respond because he didn't quite know. He was meeting her parents tonight and for sure didn't want to do it before they got to know him and he'd had a chance to talk to her parents and ask for their blessing.

CATE: HELLOOOOOOO? I NEED TO KNOW.

He had to give it to her, she was persistent. But he had the Scottish stubbornness with the red hair to prove it. He turned his phone to complete silence—no ring, no vibrate—and focused on his purchase.

"Is there a wedding band that matches this?"

Hoooo—was it getting hot in here? Sweat broke out on his upper lip. He wiped his hand across his mouth. A wedding band. Yeah, that made it even more real. But he may as well get everything at once.

And pray she said yes.

"With a gem this large, I recommend a plain band. Or perhaps a thin band encrusted with tiny diamonds?"

She was really pushing those diamonds. But maybe she had a point.

"Do you have any I can see?"

Forty minutes later, he was out the door with his pick-up receipt in-hand. He now had one week before he picked the rings up to make a good impression on Chahna's parents and get their blessing. He had to make sure he pronounced their names right. Aariv and Shahinool. Ah-reev and Shuh-newl. Ah-reev and Shuh-newl.

He could do this. *You can, Mag. She's the woman of your dreams. If you don't ask her, someone else will.* His heart curled in on itself at the thought.

He would do this.

chapter four

ico was the perfect place for her parents to meet Mag. It was also surprising that her parents had chosen it. The casual Latin restaurant offered food her boyfriend loved and an atmosphere that wouldn't be too stuffy for him. And with huge windows forming a half-circle that overlooked the water, it felt open. Like Ana had room to breathe.

Why did she need room to breathe?

Because Raj was here, too. She couldn't believe they brought him to dinner, planning on setting them up together, when she told them Maguire was coming to meet them. They didn't even bat an eye.

"I'm sure he's a lovely man," her mum said. "Of course we want to meet your friend," Papa acquiesced. "But Raj is such a handsome young man, don't you think? Such a great role model."

Blah blah blah.

Ana didn't even get a moment to herself to text Mag and give him a heads-up. Her mother didn't let her out of her sight, and any time she brought her phone out, Mum clucked her tongue. "Put it away, Chahna. It's rude to play on your phone when we have a guest."

Ana could have sworn her mother winked at her.

Maguire hadn't arrived yet, but hopefully it wouldn't be long. She did tell him six o'clock, right? She glanced at her watch. He had two minutes. Her parents counted on punctuality. In their line of work, time was money and money was time.

One minute.

Her gut churned like a hurricane. She really, really wanted her parents to fall in love with Mag as much as she had.

A warm hand sent tingles down her left arm and she relaxed. Maguire was here. She looked up and saw his warm hazel eyes studying her. She stood and wrapped her arms around his waist, leaning into him.

He was her home.

"Hi," she whispered.

He ran his thumb across her cheek. "Hi."

A throat cleared behind her. Shoot. Her parents.

And Raj.

Oh boy.

Keeping her voice hushed, she leaned in for another hug and spoke into his ear. "I didn't have time to warn you. I'm sorry."

His brows furrowed when she leaned back. Before he could voice the question in his gaze, she turned.

"Papa, Mum, this is Maguire Wilson."

Mag stepped around Ana and stretched his hand out toward her father. She knew the moment he saw Raj. His movement paused for the briefest moment.

This wasn't going to be fun.

His Adam's apple bobbed before he zeroed in on her father. "It's an honor, Mr. Kapoor." He turned to her mum and shook her hand. "I see where Ana gets her beauty."

At least her mother blushed with a giggle. He'd charmed her.

"Please," her father said, "call us by our given names."

Ana noted Papa didn't give Mag their names. Was this a test?

"Thank you, Aariv." Mag looked at Ana's mother. "And Shahinool."

Ana's eyes slid closed. Perfectly pronounced.

Papa's lips pursed, then he gave a sharp nod. One hurdle crossed.

Ana's gaze roamed over his tall figure. He'd dressed up for the occasion, too. And on a police officer's salary, she could guarantee it wasn't name brand. But he made it look ten times more expensive than Armani.

She loved that he put so much effort into making such an incredible impression on her parents.

"Maguire, this is Raj. He starred with us in our last movie." Papa laid a hand on Raj's shoulder.

She wished she could say her parents were making just as big an effort to make a good impression. Oh, they were on their best behavior, but it wasn't much of a good impression when they introduced her actual boyfriend to a man they'd hoped would become her boyfriend.

Mag seemed more hesitant when he leaned forward to shake Raj's hand, and she didn't blame him. "What a coincidence you're both in San Francisco at the same time."

Raj stood and grabbed Mag's hand. "I'm here at Aariv and Shahinool's invitation. They wanted to introduce Chahna to me."

Oh no. Ana narrowed her eyes, wishing with her whole heart she could blast him with Mag's pepper spray. *Introduce me to him?* How conceited could he be?

Maguire nodded once and glanced at Ana. She mouthed *I didn't know* and shrugged.

That hurricane in her stomach? It was a category five.

If Maguire didn't know better, he'd say this guy was here to be set up with Ana. But her parents knew she had a boyfriend, so they wouldn't have done that.

Right?

Nah. There was no way.

Mag shook Raj's hand then dropped it like it was on fire. He wanted nothing to do with this guy.

"If you will please follow me, your table is ready." The host weaved through the diners until he reached a table by the windows and presented it to them with a flourish.

Mag held Ana's chair out for her. She looked stunning. She always dressed well because of her job, but he loved it when she wore her mid-back length hair down and only the tiniest hint of makeup.

"Thank you." She kissed his cheek, leaving a hot imprint, before she sat.

Once she was comfortable, Mag looked down for a chair to take. There was none. Then Ana growled. In their ten months of dating, he'd only heard that growl one other time. Someone was about to get in trouble.

"Mum, Papa." She spoke through clenched teeth.

"It's okay, ba—Ana." No need to call her babe in front of her parents. "I can go see if we can be moved to a larger table."

She lifted her gaze to him. He could drown in those ebony eyes. "That isn't the point."

Mag looked over at Raj, whose smirk Mag would like to wipe off his face with the bristliest scrub brush he could find.

"I'm afraid when I made the reservations, I forgot Ma...Mac..."

"Maguire, Mum."

"Oh," she blushed. "Yes, of course. Maguire. I forgot you'd be here. I do apologize."

She seemed sincere in her apology, but Ana's jutted chin told him his girlfriend wasn't buying it. He didn't know her parents like she did, obviously, but he was willing to give them the benefit of the doubt.

"I'll be right back." He leaned down and kissed Ana's temple, her skin soft beneath his lips. As he straightened, he caught her small smile. He winked and went to find the host.

Mag took his time. His jaw twitched from holding back his frustration and disappointment, and he needed it to stop before he got back to the table. One week away from picking up the ring he'd bought for Ana, yet her parents acted like she was single, intent on setting her up with some guy. He rubbed his hand over his jaw, trying to work out the tension.

He prayed he could convince Ana's parents he was the one for her.

chapter five

*f*rom around the larger table they'd been moved to, thanks to Mag, Ana learned a lot about Raj as the awkward dinner continued. More than she'd wanted. And from the looks on her parents faces midway through their entrées, more than they'd bargained for.

Maybe this wasn't such a bad thing after all. Raj was talking himself out of a set-up. She squeezed Mag's hand under the table. He'd taken her hand after they finished eating their meals and had decided to let dinner settle and just talk a while before even thinking about dessert.

"Which meant, of course, Filma wanted me for their cover. Too bad they didn't want my costar," he smirked. She was sure he felt really bad. The conceited—

Her phone chimed with an incoming text. Perfect timing. She really shouldn't be so judgmental. After all, he was brought here all the way from Mumbai to be set up with her.

The watch on her wrist buzzed a moment later, notifying her of the same text. She tilted her wrist—subtly, of course—to read it. A group text from the girls. She smiled. No doubt they all wanted an update on how things were going with Mag and her parents.

"It was the best-selling cover they'd ever had."

And Raj.

She watched as her parents squirmed in their seats. Served them right, the busybodies. But she loved them and appreciated that they just wanted her to be happy. Maybe now they'd recognize that she was happy. With Maguire.

"So, Maguire," her father spoke quickly, before Raj could continue. "What do you do?"

They already knew, but that was probably the first thing that came to mind in order to stop Raj from continuing to talk about himself. Beside her, Mag straightened, pride pushing his shoulders back. Her stomach fluttered. "I'm a police officer for the San Francisco PD, sir."

Papa opened his mouth, but before any sound could come out, Raj intervened. That man was too quick-tongued. "I played an Imperial Police a couple of movies ago. Such an easy career."

Ana cocked her head. "You mean acting is easy?" Her parents might have a different opinion. Actors had to learn a lot, memorize a lot, and work with so many hard personalities.

"No, acting is difficult. I meant policing."

Oh no he didn't. "Excuse me?" Ana's muscles bunched up like an elastic.

Mag's fingers tightened around hers, but she didn't care. No way was some conceited brat going to spit on her boyfriend's career. Even her father's eyes bugged out. And Mum...she'd gone pale.

Raj waved a hand in front of his face. "The police have it very easy here. A very—how do Americans say it? Cushiony? A very cushiony job."

Was it possible for heads to explode in real-life? Because she was sure hers was about to. "I believe you mean 'cushy,'" she replied, her voice so syrupy sweet, Maguire let go of her and rested his head in his hands with a quiet, "Oh no."

Oh no was right.

"Do go on, Raj." Ana pasted the smile she used for problem clients on her face.

"No!" Her mum came to life. "I'm sure he didn't mean it the way it sounded, Chahna." Her eyes pleaded with Ana, but it wasn't until she looked at her father's face, lips pulled between his teeth, that she sat back, folding her arms across her chest.

"I meant to say it's a job where they sit in donut shops, eating fattening food and drinking coffee. 'Cushy,' as Chahna said."

Her mum was next to shove her head in her hands, muttering in Hindi. Her father glanced toward the ceiling, his lips silently moving. Beside her, Mag's shoulders were shaking suspiciously. Was he laughing?

Two brats at the table. But at least one was a loveable brat.

It was only because her parents still had to work in Bollywood and this guy was famous, with everyone bowing to his every whim, that Ana sat up tall, took a deep breath, and metered her voice.

She thought she was doing a fabulous job.

"Raj, I'm not sure you understand the difference between real life and Hollywood stereotypes. And even that stereotype is decades old." She eyed Maguire beside her, letting her appreciation for him shine before turning back to Raj. "As you can see, Mag is in top physical form. He risks his life every single day, as do all his brothers and sisters on the force, in order to serve the residents of this city."

Mag lifted his head, the laughter fading from his eyes. His lips softened into a small smile. It was the kind of smile that started tingles running up and down her arms.

"I am so proud of him and his accomplishments. And I would appreciate it if you would refrain from saying another word about my fi...boyfriend."

Yikes, that'd been close. The man she'd almost named her fiancé didn't even know she had a venue picked out. For this Christmas.

The whirling storm inside her picked up speed and ferocity.

It took a few uncomfortable minutes before the waiter brought their desserts to them after Ana's takedown of Raj.

Mag had never been so proud of her.

"Aariv and Shahinool," he took a deep breath. "I was wondering if you would like a tour of San Francisco?"

Ana's fork clattered to her plate. He did his best to ignore her. They hadn't talked about this, but he really wanted time alone with them.

"I know Ana has to work tomorrow and my shift doesn't start until later, so I have free time and would love to spend it with you both."

He purposefully left Raj out of it. Rude? Probably. Did he care? Only a little. And that was because his mam—what he'd always called his mother growing up in Scotland—had taught him to be a gentleman. Was he going to change his mind and include him? No way.

Sorry, Mam. But something told him she'd be very okay with his actions.

"Well, Maguire, that would be wonderful. Thank you." Her father nodded.

"Yes, thank you. That is very kind."

Ana's fingers brushed across the back of his hand resting on his thigh. He turned his hand over and grasped them, stroking his thumb over her soft skin. She squeezed and laid her head on his shoulder.

The receipt for her engagement ring burned a hole in his pocket.

One week.

chapter six

"*A*na, can you get those fabric samples for the Peeler account and come to my office?"

Jillian Dawson waited for no one. She expected with absolute certainty that her instructions would be followed to the letter, so Ana didn't bother to respond. She jumped away from her desk, found the sample book, and quick-paced it down the hall, her heels echoing in the minimalist office.

"Here you are, Jillian." She placed the book on the expansive desk and sat on the edge of the ghost chair, smoothing her black pencil skirt as she waited.

"Mm-hm." Jillian turned each sample, squinting at one before moving on to the next. She repeated the process several times before her long, red fingernail tapped a matte black leather. "This one." She turned her chair and plucked a thick binder off the cabinet, let it thud on her desk, and pushed it across to Ana.

"I want you to place the order for the sofas in this binder with this fabric," she pointed back at the leather. "They'll tell you it will be twelve weeks, but make sure they know it's for me, and I expect them in eight. I don't have time for their foolishness."

Jillian came across as demanding and exact—and she was—but she had a heart of gold deep down. Way deep down.

"I'm on it."

Her boss held her hand up, stopping Ana before she could stand. "Before you go, I want to talk to you about something."

Could one keep living if their heart stopped? Because Ana's heart came to a screeching halt. At least she was still breathing. Barely.

"I can't believe it!"

"I'm so proud of you. That's amazing!" Leilah's serene smile always lifted Ana's spirits, even when her spirits were already high.

Ana watched as Cate danced in her video box, Lydia and Hanady were grinning, and Ruthie...oh sweet Ruthie. Pregnant and glowing and beautiful.

"Thank you, guys. I'm completely gob smacked that Jillian handed me an account to lead. I know she'll watch over my shoulder, but still. I didn't think this would happen for another year or so."

"You've paid your dues in spades." Cate pursed her lips. "And spades. And spades."

Ana leaned back in her computer chair, staring at the screen. She loved her friends. In truth, they were more like sisters. Her heart swelled at the thought of their years of sisterhood.

She sighed. "I should go. I'm meeting Papa and Mum for dinner again. Mag had them out today, touring the Bay. I'm almost afraid to find out how it went."

"Did that guy go with them?" Lydia scowled.

"Heavens, no! He wasn't exactly great company at dinner last night—well, for the rest of us. He sure entertained himself, though. Mum texted this morning. I guess he took off down to Los Angeles today. No doubt hoping to make his mark on Hollywood."

Ana's eyes narrowed. Ruthie had started looking a little green. "Ruthie, I think the color is off on your camera."

Their friend lurched forward, slamming her hand against her mouth.

"Oh. Not the color on your camera, then."

She shook her head, muted her mic, and ducked off camera. A moment later, her head popped back up, but she still looked sick.

"Go, Ruthie," Leilah prodded. "We'll talk to you later."

She nodded and disconnected from the video chat.

"I should run, too," Cate said. "Noah should be here any minute for our date."

"Aw, have fun!" Hanady waved her fingers.

"Thanks!" With that, Cate shut her call down.

"I hate to say it, but..." Leilah grinned.

"You and Reggie have a game night planned?"

Leilah pressed her lips between her teeth. "Maybe."

"Go, Leilah," Lydia laughed. "And have fun."

"Love you girls!" And she was gone.

"Sorry, ladies. It's now my turn to bow out. I do need to get ready for dinner with my parents."

Once Ana signed off, she looked through her closet. Too bad Mag had to work. It would have been nice to have dinner just the four of them. She rummaged through her closet and chose a simple red bodycon dress and paired it with black heels. But really, all she could think about was her upcoming meal at Waterbar. Was it wrong her mouth was watering? It was a hard restaurant to get into, so she'd never been, but she'd heard all about the food from Jillian.

A glance at her watch told her it was time to get downstairs. Her parents told her to be waiting at 5:50pm. Which meant be there at 5:45. One millisecond either side would result in faces that showed enough disapproval to send Richard Dawkins himself to confession.

Sure enough, she'd barely stepped out the front door when a black limo pulled up. The driver exited the vehicle and opened the door.

"Welcome, Miss." He waved her inside.

"Hi Papa, hi Mum." Ana chimed as she slid in, the leather of the seats cool on her legs. Her cell phone chimed a text before they could respond. And again.

Then it rang.

"Honestly, Chahna. Can you not turn that contraption off while we're visiting with you?"

"Sorry, Mum. I'll turn it off." She reached into her black handbag. Hm. It was the Hôtel de Glace. Well, she couldn't exactly return that call in the presence of her parents. How fun that would be to explain. Well, I have our wedding venue reserved. I'm just waiting for Maguire to propose. Oh! Make sure you book your flight. We're just two months away!

Yes. A real party.

"I'm not complaining, I'm really not."

Mag stifled a yawn and eyed a car ahead of them that seemed to be going a little fast. He picked up the radar and tagged the car. "Sure you aren't." Shoot. Only speeding by two miles per hour. That was a hard ticket to win in court if the driver fought it. Not worth it.

Jason tapped his fingers on the steering wheel. "It's slow enough I could catch an episode of Golden Girls."

The first time his partner had copped up to watching that show, Mag spit coffee out his nose. It just wasn't a show you expected a young, male cop to watch. Jason claimed Maya made him watch it with her, but over time the truth had come out.

It was definitely Jason's choice.

A buzz on his chest drew his attention. He pulled his phone out of his shirt pocket. He didn't recognize the area code but answered it anyway.

"Hello?"

"Bonjour, may I speak with Maguire Wilson?"

French? "Speaking."

"Ah, good. Monsieur Wilson, I'm calling from Hôtel de Glace about your reservation."

"Reservation? At...where?"

"Hôtel de Glace, in Québec. The ice hotel."

"Are you sure you have the right Maguire Wilson?" He rattled off his phone number.

"Oui, I'm quite sure. You are with Chahna Kapoor, yes?"

Uh oh. Did Ana arrange a surprise trip for him? They'd never gone away together, and if they did, it'd be separate rooms. But an ice hotel? He shivered. He was a summer guy, all the way.

No matter how much he hated winter, though, he hated that her surprise was ruined even more.

Lin pulled the patrol car up outside a convenience store and put it in park. He jutted his chin toward the store and whispered, "Want anything?"

Mag shook his head. Jason nodded and climbed out of the car, leaving him to figure out whatever was going on.

"Yes, I guess you do have the right person."

"Oh good. I'm calling because part of the form Chahna filled out was illegible."

He grinned. Not surprising. Her penmanship rivaled the proverbial doctor's. "How can I help you?"

"I couldn't quite read the number of rooms you'd need."

An easy fix. Good. "Oh, only two, please."

There was silence on the other end of the phone. "I'm sorry, monsieur, but there had to be more than two. It was double-digits. I just couldn't read if the second number was five or six."

Why would they need more than two rooms? Unless her friends were going with their boyfriends and husbands.

"When is the reservation for again?"

"December 21ˢᵗ until Christmas Eve."

Uh, wow. That was cutting it close to Christmas. He wasn't planning on visiting Mam in Scotland this year—he'd planned on spending it with Ana, hopefully planning their wedding. But if she wanted to go away with her friends and take him with her, he wouldn't argue. Kind of wish she'd talked to him about it first. Sounded like an expensive vacation, but it could be fun, and he had a savings he could dip into a little bit.

He counted out her friends. He knew Ruthie would be too pregnant in December to travel. So that left Hanady and her husband, Leilah and

Reggie—would they be married by then? Then there was Cate and Noah, and Lydia. He didn't think Lydia was seeing anyone. So that was...five or six rooms. But she said double digits. Maybe Lydia was seeing someone. Even if she was, though, that still didn't make sense.

"I'm sorry...I didn't catch your name."

"Ah, my apology. I am Noémie."

"No apology necessary. Noémie, I'm only coming up with a maximum of six rooms."

"You mean 26. Okay."

"No...six. Only six."

"I'm sorry, but that is definitely a two in front of the six—or five. And I wanted to confirm, you each have two attendants in your bridal party."

Heat rushed up his neck. Bridal party? Our bridal party?

"Maybe I should try reaching Chahna again. The brides do always seem to know more than the grooms." Her musical laugh did nothing to ease the heat pulsing up his neck to his face. Bride?

"Uh, I'm sorry, Noémie. I'm sure Ana can clear this up. I'll talk to her and one of us will give you a call back."

"Thank you. Bonsoir!"

Lin pulled the door open and climbed back in. Mag knew that. But at that moment, he felt like he was having an out-of-body experience. Chahna had booked an ice hotel for their wedding? Their wedding. Did she know he was going to propose?

He eyed his partner. "Did you let it slip to Ana that I'm considering proposing?"

Jason scrunched his face. "Dude, no. That'd be violating the Bro Code."

"Do you think maybe Maya told her?"

He shook his head. "I haven't even told Maya." He pushed his fist into Mag's shoulder. "No offense, man, but when I get home and see my wife, you're the last thing on my mind to talk to her about."

Mag flopped his head back on the headrest. Yeah, he could see that.

"Why?" Jason dragged his question out. "What's going on?"

He told Lin about the call. "She said Ana was the bride and referred to me as the groom. What's going on?"

"Only one way to find out." He tapped the clock on the dash. "But we have a few hours left of the most boring shift ever before you can talk to her."

chapter seven

*W*aterbar had been well worth the wait. Ana kicked her heels off and threw her handbag onto the little table beside the door. Too bad Mag hadn't been able to join them. Her parents didn't even have another man there to set Ana up with. Apparently, their director's cousin's son in Sacramento had to cancel at the last minute. Too bad.

She huffed a laugh. No, not too bad. Not at all.

Her watch buzzed against her wrist. A text from Mag. He always seemed to know when she was thinking of him.

MAGUIRE: YOU HOME?

CHAHNA: I AM. JUST WALKED IN THE DOOR.

She looked at the time. He should have ended his shift a half-hour ago.

CHAHNA: HOW WAS WORK?

MAGUIRE: FINE. CAN I COME OVER?

It was late, but she was always up for seeing him and getting a hug, and maybe a kiss. Or two.

CHAHNA: OF COURSE! WHEN WILL YOU BE HERE?

The front door buzzer belted out its off-tune growl and she jumped. Was he really here? He must have been parking just as she walked in the front.

She pressed the button. "Mag?"

"Yep."

"Come in!"

She never tired of the electricity that zinged down her arms when she knew she was about to see him.

He knocked twice. She peered through the peephole—he'd drilled that into her when they first started dating—and slid the locks open when she saw it was for sure him.

When the door opened, she threw her arms around his neck and pressed her lips against his in a quick smack.

"I missed you."

She heard him breathe in her shampoo. He'd told her once he loved the banana and coconut smell. It reminded him of summertime at the beach.

"I missed you too. And that dress..." He moved his face to look at her. "I love that dress." He cleared his throat. "But I need to talk to you."

She pulled back at the faraway look in his eyes. Those were never good words. "What's up?"

"Can I come in?"

Oh. Right. They were still standing in her doorway. She stepped back and let him through, closing and locking the door behind him.

He sat in the corner of her dark grey sofa, his left arm stretched out across the back, and his right ankle resting on his left knee. She took it as an invitation to snuggle under his arm and lay her head on his chest.

"So, what did you want to talk to me about?"

"I got an interesting call tonight."

She rubbed her fingers across his uniform shirt. The thicker fabric wasn't terribly soft, but his steady heartbeat under her ear was comforting enough. "From who?"

"Hôtel de Glace."

Ana shot up, feeling the blood drain out of her face. Did she even dare look at him?

She licked her lips, then turned her body to face him. "Oh?" Maybe they reached out to him for a different reason?

Right, Chahna. She closed her eyes, annoyed at her own attempt to console herself. How would they have gotten his number unless they lifted it

41

from the paperwork she'd scanned and emailed? The pounding of her heart echoed in her ears.

Then she remembered they'd called her when she first got in her parent's car.

No. No, no, no!

"Yeah. She—Noémie—couldn't read the last digit you'd written when indicating the number of rooms you needed to reserve."

She couldn't swallow past the rock in her throat.

"Was it 25 or 26 rooms?"

If she stayed quiet, she couldn't incriminate herself, right?

"We each only have two bridal party members. So, who are the rest of the guests at our wedding?"

"Mag, I—"

He held up a hand, leaned forward and rested his elbows on his knees before clasping his hands together. Tightly, she noticed.

"I really—" Ana didn't get to finish before Mag interrupted her again.

"I—" he cut himself off and pierced her with a confused frown. "Were you going to propose?"

"Me?" Ana balked. That was preposterous. She was a modern, independent woman, but there was still a heavy dose of traditional in her.

"Yeah. Were you?"

"Of course not."

His shoulders lifted and dropped, a heavy breath accompanying the move. "So, what made you book an ice hotel for our wedding in two months?"

"Technically, two-and-a-half."

A cringe pinched her brows together. Wrong thing to say. But how was she to answer that? *I actually sent in the reservation request before I met you. When they called to give me the date, I just hoped you'd magically propose in the next couple of days.* Yeah, that'd go over magnificently.

"I just..."

His hazel stare slammed into her.

"When Noémie called, I really thought she meant next December. I thought that would give us plenty of time to discuss marriage, get engaged, and plan a wedding. It wasn't until her email arrived that I found out it was for two months from now."

"And you didn't explain to her because..."

Because I love you and want to be your wife. Because I believed you loved me. I still do. Because I want to start our lives together now.

She really wished her mouth would work with her brain sometimes. Instead, she sat there, lips sealed.

"I don't even know what to think, Chahna."

Her stomach dropped. He rarely used her full name. It didn't give her much hope tonight would end well.

"Mag, I love you. I just thought maybe you were close to proposing, and this is my dream venue and I didn't want to lose it."

He jumped to his feet and paced her tiny living room, his hands running through his hair.

"'Didn't want to lose it.' You didn't even talk to me about this."

"Because I didn't want to ruin any surprise proposal you might have."

He stopped and stared at her. "We'd never even talked about marriage. I was hoping to once I got to know your parents and talk to them, but..." His voice trailed off. He stood in front of her window that looked out over an alley.

"Mag, I'm sorry. I really am."

"Yeah, me too."

He stepped over to her, leaned down, and kissed the top of her head, then walked out without another word.

The door clicked shut, leaving Ana to her thoughts. Her belly knotted, knowing this was all her fault. Cate had tried to warn her.

Her boyfriend didn't want to talk, and her chest pressed against her lungs, making her feel like she couldn't breathe.

A sleepless night had Ana calling her best friend bright and early. It took a minute for Cate to be coherent, but once Ana told her what had happened, Cate was totally alert.

"I blew it, Cate."

"Nooo...I don't think you did. You said he kissed you when he left, right?"

"Yeah, but he didn't say anything."

"He's a guy. He probably just needs to process and will be right as rain by tomorrow."

"I don't know, Cate."

Her friend's sigh sounded through the phone. "I'm sorry. But he's a good man. And I'm absolutely sure he loves you."

Ana's shoulders slumped. "Does he though?"

"Don't let guilt lie to you, Ana. I know he does. You know he does."

"You sound so sure."

"I told you. I am. And you are, too."

Ana flopped down into the spot Mag held last night on her couch. And pulled the white furry blanket over her legs. She wished she had a cat to pet. Maybe she could borrow her neighbor's.

"Trust me, Ana."

"I do."

"Good. So how are you going to make this right?"

Ana ran her hand over the blanket. She had no idea what she was going to do.

JASON: YOU WERE GOING TO PROPOSE TO HER ANYWAY, RIGHT?

MAGUIRE: YEAH. BUT IT WAS KIND OF A SHOCK TO FIND OUT SHE ALREADY HAD A HOTEL RESERVED. FOR OUR WEDDING. THIS DECEMBER.

MAYA: COME ON, MAGUIRE. WHAT WAS THE HARM?

MAGUIRE: WAIT, THIS IS A GROUP TEXT?

Mag groaned. Why wouldn't it be? Jason included his wife in everything. It was really good...until it involved Mag.

MAYA: SURE IS. AND WAIT...YOU WERE GOING TO PROPOSE???

JASON: GET OVER IT. AND MAYA'S RIGHT. WHAT WAS THE HARM? AND YES, WIFEY. HE'S ALREADY BOUGHT THE RING. HE'S JUST WAITING TO PICK IT UP FROM BEING SIZED.

MAYA: WOW. AND YOU'RE MAD THAT SHE BOOKED A VENUE ALREADY?

MAGUIRE: NOTHING LIKE BEING GANGED UP ON.

JASON: GET OVER IT.

MAYA: PLAY NICE, HONEY.

JASON: DON'T HAVE TO. WHAT ARE PARTNERS FOR?

MAYA: UGH. HUSBANDS. ANYWAY, MAG, SHE JUST LOVES YOU AND WANTS TO SPEND THE REST OF HER LIFE WITH YOU. WHAT'S SO BAD ABOUT THAT?

MAGUIRE: ...

JASON: HELLO? YOU GONNA ANSWER?

MAGUIRE: I'M A SLOW TYPER.

JASON: SERIOUSLY?

MAYA: GIVE HIM A MINUTE. MAYBE HE HAS SOMETHING SIGNIFICANT TO SAY.

What was so bad about Ana wanting to spend the rest of her life with him? Nothing. With booking a wedding venue before they were even engaged? Well— He— It just was.

Wasn't it?

MAGUIRE: I DON'T KNOW.

MAYA: ...REALLY?

MAGUIRE: LOOK, I JUST HAD A PICTURE IN MY HEAD OF HOW THIS WAS ALL GONNA GO DOWN. AND I THOUGHT WE'D SPEND THIS CHRISTMAS PLANNING OUR WEDDING, DREAMING ABOUT THE FUTURE. THAT STUFF.

JASON: WELL, INSTEAD OF PLANNING YOUR WEDDING, YOU GET TO BE MARRIED.

MAGUIRE: ...

MAYA: <EYE ROLL EMOJI>

JASON: <LAUGHING WITH JOY EMOJI>

MAGUIRE: THIS ISN'T FUNNY.

MAYA: YOU'RE RIGHT. IT ISN'T. SHE'S PROBABLY HEARTBROKEN.

MAGUIRE: YOU THINK?

MAYA: OF COURSE! YOU TWO ARGUED AND HAVEN'T TALKED SINCE.

MAGUIRE: BUT I KISSED HER BEFORE I LEFT.

MAYA: YEAH, BUT YOU HAVEN'T TALKED TO HER SINCE.

MAGUIRE: IT'S ONLY 8AM.

MAYA: EXACTLY. IT'S BEEN NINE HOURS.

JASON: YOU BETTER GO MAKE THINGS RIGHT, BUDDY. OR YOU'LL NEVER GET MAYA OFF YOUR BACK.

MAGUIRE: MY WORST NIGHTMARE. ;)

MAYA: NOT FUNNY. NOW GO. FIX THIS. AND JASON...YOU'RE IN TROUBLE.

JASON: I LOVE YOU HONEY. YOU SHOULD GO SHOPPING TODAY.

MAGUIRE: OKAY, OKAY.

MAYA: AND JASON? WHERE'S THE CREDIT CARD?

Mag laughed as he closed out the messages. Those two were a great match, and he was thankful for their friendship. But were they right? Yeah. Maybe they were.

chapter eight

*A*na?"

Ana jumped at the deep voice, dropping the Peeler binder with a thud onto her desk. "Mag! What are you doing here?"

Please don't let this be a break-up scene. Please don't let this be a break-up scene!

Mag drew closer. "I'm really sorry I got so angry last night."

Her nose tingled. Now was not the time to cry. "Oh Mag. No, I'm sorry! I didn't mean to deceive you, or trick you, or do anything of the sort. I was just so excited that my dream venue was available, and I really did think it was for next year, and I just love you so much and I want to marry you and spend the rest of my li—"

She'd never been quieted with a kiss before. But she liked it.

Warmth crept up her neck. She was sure her coworkers were spying on them, but her arms had a mind of their own and slid around his waist. Adrenaline crowded her veins as he turned his head to another angle and his hands moved from her shoulders, up her neck and behind her head, cradling it like she was the most precious jewel.

Oh, the man could kiss.

"I'm so happy we don't have clients in here right now."

Ana snapped away from Mag at the icy tone of Jillian's voice. "Jillian! I'm so sorry." She slid her gaze to Mag. The insufferable man just stood there, grinning like he'd won the world championship. Which to be fair, if the sport were kissing, he'd win. By ten kilometers at least.

Jillian spared her a rare smile. "It's okay. It looks like it was a needed apology."

The boss lady knew her stuff.

"Take fifteen and go work it out in the coffee shop downstairs."

Ana nodded. "Thank you."

Mag echoed her thanks, grabbed her hand, and led her down to the coffee place she tried so hard to stay away from. Their peanut butter caramel iced coffees were to die for.

With cups in hand, they slid into a corner booth, the brown vinyl creaking as she shifted her legs all the way under the table. Maguire sat across from her, his hands wrapped around his dirty chai.

She took a deep breath. "I truly am sorry, Mag. I guess I was just hoping that you were feeling the same as me." She lowered her gaze, her cheeks flaming to life. She'd never been one to be so blunt with her feelings, especially when she wasn't entirely sure where her boyfriend stood, but after the rude surprise he'd received last night, she owed him that much.

"Ana." He waited until she looked up at him, then he reached across the table and clasped her hand. "I love you. And I can't, nor do I want to, imagine my life without you in it."

Her heart thudded. Was he about to...?

"I'm just not ready quite yet."

She was sure her heart crashed louder than a 15-car pileup on the I-5.

"I understand." At least, she could pretend she did. If he couldn't imagine his life without her in it, what was stopping him from proposing?

"Do you?"

"Yes." Who cared if her voice squeaked? She could put on a brave face. And he didn't say he wouldn't ever ask her to marry him. Just not yet.

Looked like she could kiss her dream venue goodbye for the next year or two.

Ana wasn't hiding her disappointment as well as she thought she was. Her slumped shoulders, when she usually had amazing posture—thanks to her British boarding school—said everything Mag needed to know. He hated making her feel that way, but he really wasn't ready. He'd had a great visit with her parents showing them the Golden Gate Bridge and a few other iconic places the day before, but he really needed at least one more good opportunity to show them who he was and get their blessing.

He really hoped the visit yesterday dispelled their desire to continue their matchmaking pursuits.

Mag squeezed her hand before letting go and taking a sip of his chai. He swallowed, then asked, "Are you okay?"

Ana smoothed the front of her shirt, avoiding his gaze. She didn't seem okay.

"I am." She finally looked up with a small smile. "Really."

He didn't believe her for a moment, but he didn't want to call her out on it. "Okay."

"I'll email Noémie later and cancel the reservation."

A spike of energy shot through him. "No. Uh, I know it's a disappointment for you." Think, Wilson, think. "I don't want you to have to deal with that. I have her number from last night. I'll call and talk to her."

If he was going to propose soon, and she'd been willing to hang on to the reservation in case he did, then she was obviously willing to plan a wedding on short notice. Maybe he could surprise her with this when he did finally ask her.

Ana sagged against the seat and nodded. "Thanks, Mag. I appreciate it."

That spike of energy now tingled. He needed to talk to her parents.

He walked her back up to her office before he planted another kiss on her, in front of all her coworkers, of course. Including Jillian, who just rolled her eyes and walked the opposite direction.

Mag grinned, held her smooth brown cheeks and leaned in for one last quick kiss. "I'll talk to you later, okay?"

She nodded. "Okay. Have a good shift tonight."

"I will, Lass."

As soon as he stepped outside the building and was on the street, he pulled his phone and tapped a number.

"Hello?"

"Mr. Kapoor, this is Maguire."

"Ah yes, Maguire. How are you?"

"I'm fine, sir. I was wondering if you and Mrs. Kapoor are free," he glanced at his watch and did a quick calculation, "in about forty minutes?"

A muffled voice sounded before Ana's father came back on the line. "Yes, of course. Shall we meet in the hotel?"

"That's perfect. Thank you, sir."

"Aariv is fine, Maguire. Will Chahna be joining you?"

His stomach muscles twitched. "Uh, no. It'll just be me."

It was a moment before Aariv spoke. "Okay then. We will see you downstairs in forty minutes."

Mag ended the call and looked down the street toward the bay. Her parents weren't staying here long, which was surprising considering the distance they traveled to visit, but they'd told him yesterday they had a busy filming schedule. So, unless he wanted to try to get a hold of them during filming and talk to them about something as serious as marriage to their daughter while they were focused on their movies, he needed to sit down with them.

Nausea rolled through his gut.

It was now or never.

chapter nine

Maguire strode into the lobby of the Fairmont Heritage Place and immediately saw Aariv and Shahinool Kapoor sitting side-by-side on a sofa. As soon as Aariv saw him, he stood, held his hand out to help his wife up, and nodded once at Mag.

He didn't expect it to be so hot in the lobby. Sweat broke out on his upper lip.

"Maguire, why don't we go to the rooftop terrace?"

Mag ran a finger under his T-shirt collar. It had to be cooler out there, right? "That sounds great."

Aariv led them to the bar where they ordered drinks—wine for Ana's parents, and a bottled water for himself—then they took a silent trip up the elevator to the roof.

Once they seated themselves on the outdoor chairs, Mag cleared his throat. Here went nothing.

"Mr. and Mrs. Kapoor—"

"Please," Ana's father interrupted. "Aariv and Shahinool."

"Right. Aariv and Shahinool." It was just as hot out here as it was in the lobby. The ocean breeze was doing nothing to cool his skin. He puffed his cheeks and blew the breath out. "I want you to know I love your daughter very much."

The door to the terrace opened and shut with a thud. Mag kept his focus on his (hopeful) future in-laws.

Aariv, however, didn't. He looked up at the person who'd just come through the door. "Ah, Sanjay." He glanced over at Mag. It looked like he was hot, too. Shahinool's eyes grew five times bigger.

Was this another set-up?

Really?

Aariv stood, stuffing his hands in his pockets. "Um, Sanjay." He cleared his throat. "This is Maguire Wilson, a...uh..."

He'd never heard Aariv Kapoor stammer.

"A friend of Chahna's," Aariv finished weakly.

Friend? He'd just told this man he was in love with his daughter. And he was just labeled a friend. That didn't bode well for getting their blessing.

Sanjay's gaze traveled from Mag's toes up to the top of his head, a smirk replacing the full smile he'd graced Aariv with.

Nice to meet you, Enemy Number One. He sighed. Maybe that was too strong a label.

"Of course. A friend only." He eyed Mag again. "Obviously."

What was that supposed to mean? Sounds like that label wasn't too strong.

Sanjay took Shahinool's hand and kissed the back of it before yet again studying Mag. This guy was too much.

"Sit, sit." Aariv motioned to the chair beside Mag.

The four of them sat, traffic noise from the streets below filling the silence.

"So, Maguire. What were you saying?"

Right. Like he was going to get into it in front of this Sanjay.

He steadied himself with a breath through his nose. "It can wait." Not really, but what could he do? "Maybe another time."

Shahinool smiled. "Of course."

"I should really go. My shift starts soon." Technically he still had a couple of hours, but they didn't need to know that.

Aariv stood and held out his hand. "Thank you for coming to see us. Will you be joining us for dinner tomorrow evening?"

Ana had mentioned that earlier. Thankfully, it was a day off. Though she'd be there, it might still work to have a few minutes alone with her parents. "Yes, sir."

"Good," said Shahinool. "We'll see you then."

He really didn't like that there was another guy weaseling his way in with Ana's parents. C'mon, man. Don't think the worst. They didn't confirm he was there to be introduced to Ana. Maybe they just called Mag "friend" because they...nope. He couldn't come up with a reason for that.

He'd just have to wait until tomorrow night.

CATE: HOW'D IT GO WITH MAG?

CHAHNA: THANKFULLY, ALL'S FORGIVEN. HE'S TAKING CARE OF CANCELLING THE HOTEL. HE FELT BAD MAKING ME DO IT.

CATE: HE'S CANCELING IT? REALLY?

CHAHNA: WELL YES. WE AREN'T ENGAGED. WHAT'S THE POINT OF KEEPING IT?

CATE: I JUST THOUGHT...

CHAHNA: I'D HOPED.

CATE: HUH. WELL...MAYBE HE'LL ASK YOU SOON AND THE HOTEL WILL STILL BE AVAILABLE? OR MAYBE YOU CAN GET IT FOR NEXT YEAR.

CHAHNA: I DOUBT IT. THEY BOOK SO FAR OUT. GETTING IT THIS YEAR WAS LUCKY.

CATE: MAYBE LUCK HAD NOTHING TO DO WITH IT.

CHAHNA: ...I KNOW. BUT IF IT WAS SOMETHING GOD PROVIDED, THEN MAG WOULD HAVE ALSO ASKED ME TO MARRY HIM. HE DIDN'T. I THOUGHT HE MIGHT WHEN WE TALKED EARLIER TODAY, BUT NADA.

CATE: YOU NEVER KNOW. HE MIGHT SURPRISE YOU.

CHAHNA: DOUBTFUL. HE TOLD ME HE 'WASN'T QUITE READY.'

CATE: ARE YOU OKAY?

CHAHNA: I WILL BE.

CATE: YOU BETTER PUT A RING ON IT.

MAGUIRE: UH...OKAAAAAY.

CATE: SERIOUSLY. ARE YOU REALLY CANCELLING THE HOTEL?

MAGUIRE: YOU TALKED TO ANA.

CATE: OF COURSE I TALKED TO ANA. WE'RE BEST FRIENDS. WE TALK.

MAGUIRE: TRUST ME, CATE.

CATE: ARE YOU GOING TO ASK HER???

MAGUIRE: NOT YET.

CATE: WHY?

MAGUIRE: ALL CAPS AREN'T NECESSARY, YOU KNOW.

CATE: THEY ARE WHEN I NEED TO KNOW WHY?

MAGUIRE: UGH. BECAUSE. I WANT TO GET HER PARENTS' BLESSING.

CATE: ...OH. WELL. THAT'S ACTUALLY SWEET.

MAGUIRE: I KNOW.

CATE: IF ONLY YOU COULD SEE ME ROLLING MY EYES.

MAGUIRE: BUT I BET YOU'RE LAUGHING.

CATE: I REFUSE TO COMMENT. HAVE YOU TALKED TO HER PARENTS YET?

MAGUIRE: NO. I TRIED, BUT WE GOT INTERRUPTED BY SOME DUDE NAMED SANJAY.

CATE: WHO'S THAT?

MAGUIRE: COULDN'T TELL YA. I LEFT. WE'RE HAVING DINNER WITH THEM TOMORROW NIGHT. HOPEFULLY I'LL GET A CHANCE THEN.

CATE: JUST BE PATIENT. I'M SURE IT'S COMING.

CHAHNA: PROBABLY. JUST NOT SOON.

CATE: PATIENCE, SWEET FRIEND.

Ana closed the text app and placed the phone on the arm of her sofa. She grabbed Ronie Kendig's latest novel, a space opera that she was devouring, pulled her blanket over her, and relaxed into the soft cushion. Cate was probably right. He would ask her to marry him. Eventually. She just had to be patient.

She opened her copy of Brand of Light and settled into the problems of another world.

chapter ten

A dinner party wasn't what she was expecting. Ana looked around the private dining area and recognized only Mag, whom she was of course with, and her parents, though one person from what looked to be a couple was familiar. That couple was talking to her parents, two older men in a corner discussing something that had them quite animated, and...oh no. No, please no. A single man about her age, maybe a little older, who was studying her with approval in his eyes.

Her parents better not have ulterior motives for inviting this guy.

"Maguire, Chahna." Her mum moved toward them with her arms outstretched. She hugged Ana, then gave a pat on Mag's arm before stepping back to talk. "I'm so happy you could make our little gathering."

What did they expect? They were leaving tomorrow. She really thought this was a family-only dinner.

"I wouldn't have missed it, Mum."

"Good. Now, there are several people I want you to meet." Shahinool turned to face the room. "Over there in the corner are Max Warbly and Aaron Pith. Both executive producers." She moved her hand in front of her mouth and lowered her voice. "Your father and I aren't big fans, but they're important people and we have an idea we want to run past them." She straightened. "The couple your papa is speaking to is Chadwick and Natalie Jackson. Natalie is a model."

Ah, That was why the woman was familiar. Ana studied the tall African American. She had model written all over her. When their gazes met, the warmth in Natalie's eyes put Ana at ease. Natalie smiled, and focused back on Papa once Ana returned her smile.

"And this," Mum waved the single man over. "This is Sanjay. Remember, I told you about him?"

Mag's arm around her shoulders tensed.

"I don't remember you mentioning his name." And yes. This was another not-so-subtle introduction. She tried prying her clenched teeth apart, but it was no use.

She really needed a mouthguard.

"Oh, maybe I didn't tell you his name. But I'm sure I told you about my director's cousin's son in Sacramento." She flashed her movie star smile, but Ana noticed it didn't quite reach her eyes. Maybe she was feeling uncomfortable.

Good.

Ana watched Sanjay as he very obviously smirked at Mag. What was his deal?

Sanjay reached for Ana's hand. Oh, how she wanted to be rude, but her mum's pleading eyes defeated her rudeness. She allowed him to take her hand, but the moment he started to bend as if to kiss it, she shook it.

Exaggeratingly so.

"Nice to meet you, Sanjay." She pulled her hand out of his grasp and placed it on Mag's chest. "This is my fi—" Shoot! She'd almost done it again. "—boyfriend, Maguire Wilson."

Mag either didn't notice the plea in her mum's eyes or chose to ignore it. He didn't stick out his hand, didn't say a word. Just glared.

Her boyfriend was a very astute man if he'd picked up on this scheme.

A door to the private dining area opened and the hostess of the restaurant stepped through. "Dinner is served." She stepped aside and three waiters came through the door bearing trays of food.

Her father cleared his throat. "I hope you don't mind, but I took the liberty of ordering for our little group."

One of the waiters emptied a tray of plates bearing tantalizing Indian food. He began pointing them out. "This is Dahi Puri." He explained what it was, then motioned to another plate. "This is saffron brioche Pao—my personal favorite. And this," he pointed to a third set of plates, "is pomegranate-glazed barbeque pork ribs with toasted hempseed and pink peppercorn."

Ana tried her best to be subtle when she ran two fingers across her mouth to check for drool, but subtle wasn't her gift. Beside her, Mag laughed under his breath.

Such a brat.

Another waiter laid more plates on the table. "We invite you to taste this traditional butter chicken with red pepper makhana, cashews, cilantro, and fenugreek. We also have lamb shank nihari with fresh ginger, rose, cilantro, and a chili oil."

Would it be considered uncouth if she nosedived onto the table with her mouth open, and gobbled all the food up?

The other waiter laid out both plain and garlic naan, saffron rice, and a chickpea curry.

She'd died and gone to heaven.

There was definitely enough food on the table to feed the nine people in the room and all of heaven.

Mag leaned in and placed his mouth close to her ear. "You aren't the only one drooling."

She side-eyed him in time to see him cover his own mouth with his hand and wipe. He winked at her, then the small of her back warmed as he laid his hand there and motioned toward the table.

As the others began to dig into the food, Mag grasped her hand under the table and once more leaned toward her. His hot breath fanned her ear as he whispered. "Father, thank you for this food, for this time with Ana and her parents. Please bless this food to our bodies as Your Word nourishes our soul. Amen."

"Amen." How she loved a man that led.

The guy really did need to put a ring on her finger or she would be forced to buck tradition and propose to him.

Conversation flowed throughout the meal. Ana's father sat at the head of the table with her mum to his right and Ana to his left. Beside Ana was, of course, Mag. But beside her mum was Sanjay.

He'd behaved himself over dinner, but as dessert was being served—she'd ordered the Mawa Burfi, a butter biscuit with warm chocolate and chikki gelato—his focus zeroed in on her.

Ugh.

A waiter sat Mag's dessert in front of him. He picked up his spoon, but Ana was faster and dug her own spoon into his Rasmalai before he could. The sweet dessert made of almond Chantilly, mango peach granita, and ice milk made her groan. Sooo good.

She spied Mag's spoon heading for her own dessert. Thrusting her hand out to protect it, she glared at him. "Don't you dare."

"But you just took some of mine!"

She jutted her chin. "I don't share my dessert. You know this."

"But..."

Narrowing her eyes, she leaned toward him and lowered her voice. "Mine."

His eyes sparkled and before she knew it, he'd pecked her lips. "You had a spot of my dessert on the corner of your mouth." He winked.

Ana rolled her eyes. He was insufferable. And she loved him fiercely.

Across the table, Sanjay cleared his throat. When she looked over at him, he was glaring at Mag.

He opened his mouth and inserted his foot. "What right do you have to kiss Chahna?"

Whoa boy.

"Excuse me?" Mag's shoulders tensed, his back stick straight.

Everyone at the table quieted.

She now knew what the phrase 'you could cut the tension with a knife' meant.

"What right do you have to kiss Chahna?"

The ginger five o'clock shadow framed tightly sealed lips. Mag glanced at her father before drawing a long breath through his nose.

Ana slid her eyes shut and squeezed Mag's thigh beneath the table.

"Her parents brought me here to meet Chahna with the intention of seeing if she's good enough for me to marry."

Oh no he didn't.

Papa bristled at that one and opened his mouth, but no sound came out. When he was so angry he couldn't get his voice to work, their guests ducked their heads and ate in silence.

Sanjay, however, didn't see the writing on the wall.

He faced her father and, not recognizing what was going on, spoke. "Please tell him, Aariv." He glanced at Ana. "And your daughter. Their behavior is appalling, and I will not have it."

For a man who was likely born right there in California, whose parent lived and worked in Los Angeles, and whose cousin-or-whatever-relation was a director in Bollywood, he was—well, Ana didn't know what to say about him. She'd met some traditional Indian families, but never did they have attitudes like this. He was downright— No, she still didn't have words to describe him. At least not ones God would be happy with her saying.

Whoa. Mag was too stunned to think beyond the single word.

Actually, no. He could think of much stronger reactions, but few were appropriate in polite company. Where did the guy come off thinking he could act this way? And toward Ana and her parents? He could handle the guy taking that attitude with him, but toward the woman he loved and his future in-laws? Because he was going to marry her.

He watched Aariv out of the corner of his eye and became concerned. The man was practically turning purple with his outrage. Shahinool sat there slack jawed. Everyone else at the table had eyes the size of their dessert plates.

It was up to him.

Mag took a steadying breath. Then another. And a third for good measure. "Sanjay." He waited until the guy looked at him. "I won't tolerate you speaking so disrespectfully to and about Ana."

Sanjay's eyes narrowed. He opened his mouth, but Mag stood, hoping he cut an imposing figure.

"And I won't have you disrespecting her father and telling him what to do."

Aariv's skin was losing the purple hue. Thank goodness. Aariv eyed him with what Mag hoped was admiration. Or at least respect.

"You've had a delicious meal at the invitation of Aariv and Shahinool, but for the sake of a peaceful time with their daughter before they leave tomorrow, I think it's time for you to say goodbye."

Sanjay jumped up from his seat, fists on the table, and leaned toward Mag. "Who do you think you are? She," he pointed at Ana, "was offered to me as a potential wife. I have every right—"

"No!"

Everyone at the table jumped at Aariv's outburst, but he didn't continue. Unfortunately, that purple hue he'd started to lose was returning. Mag needed to step it up.

"If you don't leave right now, as an officer for the San Francisco police, I'll have no choice but to arrest you for public disturbance."

Okay, so that was stretching it. Sanjay really wasn't at the public disturbance level, but maybe he didn't know that.

"Whatever." Sanjay slid his hands over his hair then looked at Aariv. "I don't want to be part of a family where they have no control over their daughter."

Mag really didn't want the police called on him, but the blood in his veins was hot and ready to boil over. He released his clenched fists and shoved both hands into his pockets to resist temptation.

"I'm out."

They all watched as Sanjay pushed back from the table and walked out, breathing a proverbial collective sigh when he was out of sight.

Mag sat back down and sipped his water. He needed it to cool down.

"Maguire."

He stopped midway to his second sip and faced Aariv. Man, he hoped he hadn't overstepped. Aariv's face was back to its normal rich brown, and the knuckles wrapped around his own water glass weren't white.

"Thank you."

Those two simple words put out the remaining fire. "It's my honor, sir."

A small smile graced Aariv's mouth. The guests at the other end of the table went back to their conversations, but Shahinool and Aariv remained quiet.

Ana rested her head on his shoulder. "I didn't think I could love you more than I already did. But I do."

He kissed the top of her head and wrapped his arm around her shoulders, brushing his fingers across the sleeve of her dress.

Ana stood on her toes and reach up to kiss his cheek. "I'll be right back. I need the restroom."

He nodded and watched as she walked off before glancing at the still-quiet Aariv and Shahinool.

Maybe now was the perfect opportunity...

chapter eleven

He didn't enjoy throwing up, but he was so nauseous right now that it'd be best to just get it over with. Mag moved to Ana's chair, glanced over his shoulder to make sure she wasn't on her way back yet, then faced her parents.

"Mr. and Mrs. Kapoor—"

"Aariv and Shahinool. We've told you." The gentle smile softened Shahinool's words.

Mag grinned. "Aariv and Shahinool. I want you to know I love Chahna. Deeply."

"Not only love but respect her." The corners of Aariv's mouth tilted up. "And her mother and I. Thank you, Maguire."

"It was my honor, sir." Mag cleared his throat. "I know Ana and I haven't been dating long."

"Six or seven months, yes?"

He smiled at her mother. "Almost ten."

Shahinool nodded. "Right. Please, I didn't mean to interrupt." She glanced at her husband then back at Mag, winking. She knew! She knew what he was about to do.

In an instant, the rolling in his belly stilled.

"With our busy schedules," he waved his hand indicating himself and them, "I know we haven't gotten to know one another as well as I would like.

But I'm hoping that can change in the future." His chest rose. "Aariv, Shahinool, I—" he looked over his shoulder. Still no Ana. He turned back to her parents. "May I have your blessing to ask Ana to be my wife?"

Shahinool pulled her lips between her teeth, her eyes shining with unshed tears. Aariv cleared his throat and shifted in his seat.

Shahinool seemed happy, but Aariv—

Maybe this was too soon. Her father wasn't happy. He didn't seem to be anything. His face gave no indication as to what he was thinking.

The nausea was back.

Aariv thrummed his fingers on the table. That couldn't be a good sign.

"Maguire, you are right. You haven't been dating our daughter for long. Nor have we had the opportunity to settle our schedules and spend time getting to know you."

Nope. Not good.

So, dying of a broken heart was a real thing. If he didn't get their blessing, he was afraid he'd have the same fate.

"That has been our mistake."

His breath caught in his chest at Aariv's words.

Aariv glanced at Shahinool. She didn't say anything or move, but it seemed something was communicated between them before he turned back to face Mag.

"It is clear to us that our daughter loves you. And even more clear that you love her. Do you believe you can provide a good life for her?"

His entire body tingled. "Yes, sir. I'll love, honor, and protect her for the rest of my life."

Aariv didn't speak right away. The clacking of heels on the tiled floor set Mag's heart hammering. Aariv's gaze slid up and over Mag's shoulder, then back to Mag.

"Absolutely."

Absolutely. Did that mean—? He stared at Aariv, who reached out and patted the back of Mag's hand once.

"Yes." He grinned at Mag.

"Yes what?"

Ana's sweet, musically accented voice floated over his shoulder.

"We've decided we need to be more present," Aariv grabbed Shahinool's hand, "and less busy. We should start with more regular video calls, yes?"

All the tension seeped out of Mag's body. Aariv didn't lie, but he didn't spill the beans, either.

Ana leaned forward and kissed Aariv's cheek. "That sounds wonderful, Papa."

More time to get to know his for-sure future in-laws? It sounded great to him, too.

In the four days since her parents flew back to Mumbai, Ana had already FaceTimed with them twice. She thought it'd be a chore, but her parents asked more questions, especially about Mag, and had called once when they were hiking up Twin Peaks. Mag had seemed disappointed they called during their hike, but he'd been happy talking with them and turning the camera out so they could see the view of the Bay Area from there.

Today he was taking her to hike along the Land's End Trail. Ana tied a teal-colored sweatshirt around her waist after dressing in black leggings and a white tank top. She threw her hair up in a messy bun, sure the ocean breeze would tangle her mid-back length hair, then slipped into her running shoes.

Her phone buzzed.

MAGUIRE: I'M HERE, LASS.

CHAHNA: BE RIGHT DOWN.

Ana grabbed her water bottle and keys, locked her door behind her, and hurried down the stairs. Exiting onto the street, she searched for Mag's car, an older Saturn Vue SUV.

Once she was in the car, she leaned over and planted a kiss on his full lips.

"How was your shift last night?"

"Good, but busy. A domestic dispute and an accident."

Two of his most hated calls. Ana ran her hand along his shoulder and squeezed. "I'm sorry. Were they bad?"

Domestic disputes and accidents were always bad. But were they bad was their code phrase to ask about injuries without tempting him to violate any privacy issues.

"The dispute wasn't 'bad.' It's amazing how alcohol can affect people, though. Thankfully, neither was the accident. Just lots of property damage."

Ana slid her eyes shut and took a moment to pray for both situations and the people involved. Mag kept quiet, knowing her routine.

She whispered, "Amen," and changed the subject to take his mind off of work. "I can't believe we're going on a second hike this week." She wrinkled her nose. "Are you trying to turn me outdoorsy?"

The smile he cracked barely lifted his lips. Hm. His left knee bounced, something he only did when he was nervous. But what would he have to be nervous about?

Wait. No. Was he? No. He hadn't even brought up marriage since their fight. She suspected he wanted to get her parents' blessing before he asked. He would have had plenty of time when he took them on the tour around San Francisco, but they barely knew each other, and it wasn't like he'd had time to talk to them after that. Unless they'd been FaceTiming with him, too.

Was it possible?

Mag parked the car in the lot at Point Lobos Avenue overlooking the Sutro Baths, burned down ruins of an over 100-year-old Greek-style bathhouse.

"Ready?" He looked over at her but didn't quite meet her gaze.

The boy was acting suspicious, setting a swarm of butterflies flittering around her stomach.

"Ready."

They took the stairs down and hung a right to get onto the Land's End Trail. The coastal path was stunning—and windy. She was thankful she brought her sweatshirt. It was hovering around 70-degrees, but the wind sent chills down her arms. She untied the oversized sweatshirt and lifted it over her head, settling it to ensure it covered her rear.

Hand-in-hand they walked along the trail, taking their time.

"Are you okay, babe?" Maybe she shouldn't have asked in case she ruined his intention of proposing. If he was going to propose. But she couldn't seem to help herself.

"Uh, yeah. Totally fine. Why wouldn't I be?"

"You just seem off."

"I do?"

She hoped to repeat that 'I do' in two months. Her heart fell remembering that he'd cancelled the hotel.

When she didn't answer, he finally looked at her. "Are you okay?"

"What? Oh, yes. Of course." And she was. She was here with the man she loved, in one of Creation's gems. Other than a ring making it a permanent connection, what more could she want?

They walked past a few lookout points, taking selfies along the way. Ana sent a couple to the girls and smiled at their responses.

Mag led her to the left and soon the trail branched. Where in the world was he taking her? They walked down some stairs that would certainly be a trial to climb back up. She sure hoped there was another way back to the car. They walked past more stairs and the trail thinned.

"Mag? Is this safe?" Ana glanced over the drop off. "It's, um, pretty steep."

He looked over his shoulder at her and smiled. "Here," he reached his hand back. "I've got you."

Don't swoon, don't swoon. If you swoon, you'll die. She looked over the drop off again. Yeah. She'd die for sure.

Waves crashed against the rocks framing a flat area. Several loose rocks also seemed to be set in a patten across the space, with something in the middle. With something in the middle.

"What's this?"

Mag looked up and waved. When Ana followed his gaze, she could have sworn she saw someone familiar pull back. "Was that Jason?"

He didn't answer, instead pulling her along behind him until they reached the edge of the pattern.

"Welcome to the Land's End Labyrinth."

The Golden Hour—when the sun was setting over San Francisco casting a golden glow over the area—highlighted the rocks forming the circular pattern. And right there in the narrow center, the light reflected. Ana covered her eyes with her hand. It looked like a bottle of wine.

Oh. My. Goodness. This had to be it. Her heart raced like she'd just finished a 400-meter sprint. She followed Mag through the maze to the center. There were no other people around, the breeze pushed the water against the shoreline, and yes. A bottle of—she glanced down—champagne, and two glasses.

"Mag..." her voice came out breathy.

He faced her and gathered her other hand into his, now holding both. "Ana, I love you."

This was it! She bit down on the inside of her lip in order to keep the squeal fighting to get out inside.

"Each day since I've known you, those feelings have only grown. But I know that feelings can come and go. There may be days in our future where we don't like each other very much or are tired and just want to be alone."

She scrunched her nose above her beaming smile. This was a weird proposal.

Then Mag knelt on one knee, which had to hurt since he was wearing shorts and this wasn't exactly a soft sand beach like in the tropics.

"Whether those feelings come or go, I choose to love you in word and deed. To make you feel safe. To make you feel respected and cherished and listened to. To be your sounding board and best friend. To be present each day."

There were no drop offs here, so it was safe to swoon, right?

"Chahna Kapoor, will you do me the honor of becoming my wife?"

Yes, yes, YES!

"Please say something, Lass."

Oh. She hadn't answered out loud? "Yes." Her voice squeaked, so she coughed to clear it and yelled. "Yes!"

Mag jumped onto both feet and swooped her into his arms, swinging her in the air before laying a long kiss on her lips. When he leaned back, he looked up and shouted, "She said yes!"

"No kidding!"

Ana looked over and up. Sure enough, Jason stood there with his phone in-hand, grinning. Maya stood beside him, hands cupped over her mouth, bouncing on her toes.

"Congratulations, you two!" Maya shouted down.

Mag stood there, holding her and grinning.

"Hey moron," Jason shouted.

Mag's brows furrowed. "What was that for?"

"Did you even give her the ring?" he laughed.

"Shoot! Right!" He scrambled back down onto one knee, reached into the pocket of his shorts and pulled out a box. He opened it, then turned it to face her.

A gasp joined the tears trailing down her cheeks. It was the most gorgeous ring she'd ever seen. He pulled the pear-cut aquamarine ring set in rose gold out of the box and slid it on her finger. The gem was surrounded by two smaller oval-cut diamonds on either side. How Mag had gotten her dream ring wasn't really beyond her—she had the best group of friends a girl could dream of, and she was sure at least one of them had helped Mag, probably Cate.

"Babe, it's breathtaking." She leaned down and kissed him. "Thank you."

He stood, framed her face with his hands, drew her close and whispered, "Chahna Tanvi Kapoor-soon-to-be-Wilson, I love you."

chapter twelve

*Y*es! His partner got it all, so as soon as I can, I'll send you the link to the video." Ana grinned at her friends. They were as excited as she was when Mag first proposed.

"He'll be here any minute, so I'll ask him when he thinks that will be. He said Jason would probably upload it to Dropbox and share the file from there."

"Have you talked dates?" Leilah had her own wedding coming up.

"Probably next year. He knows the Hôtel de Glace is my dream venue."

"As of a year ago," Hanady laughed.

She shrugged. "Still my dream venue." She couldn't keep her laugh in. "But they book a couple of years out, so if he insists on getting married there, it's going to be a long engagement."

"Chin up, buttercup." Cate leaned toward her camera. "Maybe the date they gave you is still available? Who else in their right mind would agree to a wedding two months out?"

"It's the Hôtel de Glace, Cate. Probably anyone and everyone would jump at the chance."

When Mag had dropped her off at her apartment the night before, it crossed her mind to call the hotel and see if December 23rd was still available, but there really wasn't any hope. Mag hadn't mentioned the hotel since he said he'd cancel it for her, and the last thing she wanted to do was bring up a sore spot, especially after such a beautiful night.

"I'll be okay. The only thing that really matters is that I marry Mag."

"And wear the tiara," Leilah said.

"A snowflake tiara deserves to be worn at Christmas," she sighed. "And I really don't want to wait until next Christmas to marry him so I can wear it. So," she shrugged, "looks like I'll be a spring or summer bride."

"I don't know, Ana. You look like a Christmas bride to me."

She loved Lydia.

Two knocks, a pause, and one more knock sounded on her door. "Mag's here! Love you guys."

"Keep us posted," Leilah called before Ana signed off.

She peered through the peephole and unlocked everything to open the door. "Hi babe." She wrapped her arms around his waist and laid her head on his chest, relishing his warm strength.

"Hi Lass." He kissed the top of her head. "Ready to do some wedding talk?"

She leaned back to look up at him. "More than."

Mag entered, toed off his shoes, and hung his light jacket on the hook by her front door.

"Want a drink?"

"I'll just get some water."

"Ugh."

"What?"

"You're so healthy. I really wanted coffee." Ana fluttered her lashes.

The laugh Mag offered up was deep, showering her with giddiness. She'd get to hear that laugh the rest of her life.

"Do you have Chai?"

"Am I Indian?"

He just shook his head and moved to her sofa while she went to work making their drinks.

71

Ana sat the mugs on the glass coffee table, picked up the wedding planner she'd bought on her lunch break, and nestled into Mag's side.

"We should probably talk dates first, huh?"

"Yes. Oh! Have you talked to your mum?"

He shook his head. "I figured we could call her in," he glanced at his watch, "two hours. Mam wakes up at five o'clock for work. Two hours will give her time to get out of the shower."

"Okay." Her nerves popped. She'd spoken to his mum several times, absolutely loved Lynda, and was confident Lynda loved her. But that didn't mean she'd be happy to hear they were engaged, at least not after only ten months of dating.

"I know the Hôtel de Glace is your dream venue—"

"I don't want to wait over a year to marry you." She backed away from him so he could see she was being genuine. "I'm okay if we don't get married there. I'd rather marry in the spring or summer than wait another year."

"But—"

"No buts." She opened the planner on her lap. "I haven't had time today to look at what venues might be available six to eight months out, but—"

"Ana."

"—I'm sure I can find something. Maybe—"

"Ana," he spoke a little louder.

She stopped flipping the pages and looked up. "Oops," she ducked with a grin. "Sorry. I have a one-track mind."

"No kidding, Lass. But listen," he reached for her hands.

Ana let go of the planner and took hold of him. "What?"

He pressed his lips together before blowing out a breath. "I didn't cancel the hotel."

"It's okay, I really don't nee—wait. What?"

Now it was his turn to look sheepish. "I didn't cancel it."

"You mean..."

"I mean, if you want to get married in two months, it's ours."

He...the hotel... What?! Ana jumped forward, wrapping her arms around his neck and knocking her forehead against his nose in the process, but she didn't care.

Mag had just gifted her with her dream venue.

Mag had known since the moment he met her that Ana was a strong woman. Her quiet, determined, no-stopping-me attitude proved that to him over and over the past ten months. But the sore nose, arms squeezing the breath out of him and the shriek that accompanied it after he'd told her their wedding would be in two months left no doubt.

The woman was a beast.

"Can't...breath."

His fiancée jumped back, hands covering her mouth. "Oops. Sorry, babe! I don't want to kill you before I marry you."

"Does that mean you want to kill me after you marry me?"

She punched his arm. Okay, maybe not a beast when she wasn't in shock. The unexpected punch barely moved his shoulder. "I never want you to die. Never."

"Well I haven't found the fountain of youth, so..."

Ana rolled her eyes, her mouth moving silently. She picked the planner off the floor where it had fallen when she jumped on him and opened it to the countdown checklist.

"We are so behind."

"Does that mean you want to keep the date?"

"Does the sun shine?"

Mag looked out the window of her living room. The one that faced an alley. "I can't tell."

She followed his gaze then turned and punched him again. He couldn't help the laugh.

"Anyway," she stressed the word, "we have a lot to catch up on."

"Like what? Don't we just show up, I walk out and you walk down an aisle, and a pastor marries us, and that's it?"

Ana stared at him, not saying a word.

"Well, don't we?" He was serious. He'd never been part of a wedding, though he'd gone to a few. But only as a guest, and he was an only child, so he'd never had any part in planning a wedding.

Ana's chest rose and fell in a deep sigh. "I need my girls."

She reached for her MacBook, opened FaceTime, and called the girls. Ruthie, Hanady, Leilah, Cate, and Lydia all answered. Ana had probably asked them to be on standby because he was wedding dumb.

Mag sat back, his arm stretched out behind Ana as she told her friends about the hotel. He had no idea women could have such high-pitch screeches. Nor did he know how quickly and easily this group of women could get down to work.

"Mag, first, I'm proud of you for not cancelling that hotel. Second, have you ever been fitted for a tux?" Leilah asked.

"That's a negative." Mag shook his head.

"So, you have no idea where to go?"

"Again, that's a negative. But I'm sure I can find somewhere."

"Already have a place." Ana wrote a website on a notecard and passed it to him. "Get out your phone and go to this link. Since it's after hours, no one will answer a call, but if you submit a request online, they'll call tomorrow and book your appointment."

Should it frighten him how on the ball she was with this? But he did as he was told as the women continued to talk.

"Invitations, Ana. It's too late to send them out." Cate tapped her lips with her fingers. "I know it's not at all traditional, but time is short. You'll need to send out evites."

Mag looked up from the form he was filling out on his phone to the boxes of faces staring at him from Ana's MacBook. "What are evites?"

The ladies all stopped talking and zeroed their focus in on him. Cate—she was an actual wedding planner if he remembered right—answered. "Electronic invitations. There are several sites we can use to design and email the invites." She looked back at Ana. "Why don't I take care of that for you?"

"Oh Cate. Are you sure?"

Mag chuckled at the relief oozing from Ana's voice.

"I'm on it," Cate said confidently. "I'm going to mute myself while I search online. I'll send you a few options—and be forewarned, they will be Christmas themed."

"I wouldn't have it any other way. You're the best!" Ana said.

"Send me a guest list as soon as you can."

Ana sent Cate a thumbs-up.

"What's your budget?" Lydia asked.

Ana glanced at Mag, her cheeks pinking. "Well...my parents have always expected to be traditional and pay for my wedding, so this has come up in conversation. A lot."

"And?" This from Hanady.

"It's, um...unlimited."

Maybe it should frighten Mag how quiet this group of women could get. But this time, he too was stunned into silence.

"What does that mean?" he asked.

"They've set aside two hundred." She wasn't meeting his gaze. Neither were her friends.

Two hundred didn't seem like a lot of money for a wedding, but how much could they cost? A thousand? Five thousand? But she said it was unlimited.

Ana continued. "They've said they would spend as much as it took, though, so if it goes over two hundred..."

Mag cut in. "I'm no expert, but I'd imagine a wedding will cost more than two hundred dollars."

Leilah sucked in a breath while Hanady hid her mouth and Lydia looked down. Cate was the only one not reacting, but she was so focused on her job, she probably wasn't even listening.

"Well, um..." Ana stammered. A rare thing. "I meant two hundred...thousand." She whispered the last word, so he was sure he didn't hear right.

"Sorry, what?"

She bit her lip and looked up at him. "Thousand. Two hundred thousand."

Nope. Mag couldn't comprehend what she just said. That was an impossible number when it came to a wedding.

He sat there, unable to focus his swirling thoughts, let alone words. But it didn't matter. The girls had started talking again.

"Leilah," Ana's voice softened. "You'll come, won't you?"

He peered at the screen, waiting for her answer. Leilah was shy about her wheelchair, and he knew it was hard to travel. Put that together with going to an ice hotel in a different country, and he wouldn't be surprised if she didn't. Not to mention her own wedding.

"I...let me talk to Reggie. That's so close to our wedding."

Ana's shoulders dropped, but her voice stayed cheerful. "I totally understand if you decide you can't."

Leilah's eyes darted to him and back to Ana. "Thanks, girl. You know I love you."

"I do."

All their faces spread with grins.

"Yes, you will 'I do'!" Hanady's statement made them all laugh.

The next hour-and-a-half was spent going through the checklist, seeing what could be left off and what was essential to do. Thankfully, they'd decided to keep it small, especially with it being in Canada and so close to Christmas. But they still needed to talk to Ana's parents and give them the news.

Mag's stomach twisted. He really, really hoped they'd be okay with such a short engagement.

chapter thirteen

Your name is on the wedding account, Chahna. Your mum and I have removed ourselves, so it is solely your money now."

She knew her jaw was hanging open but seriously. Two hundred thousand dollars, all hers? "Papa, I don't know what to say. I expected you and Mum to stay on the account with me."

"Why? You're an adult and have done well for yourself, even if you didn't follow the path we'd had for you."

If listening to her papa's bemoaning a few times was the price to pay for this amazing gift, she could handle it.

"Have you set a date yet?"

Her stomach clenched. This was it. She'd hoped to do it with Mag by her side for support, but he'd asked her straight up.

"Y-yes."

"Ah, good. Your mum will be thrilled. What is the date? And do you have a venue?"

"Uh...December 23rd. At the Hôtel de Glace, just outside Québec City, in Canada."

She waited for the explosion.

"Oh...I'm guessing the very colorful flowers will be out of season. Why don't your mum and I have flowers flown in from here? It will be our gift to you."

Well. That was quite the 'explosion.' Her pulse slowed to a more normal level.

"Papa, that is so generous. I really thought you'd be upset with our date. But it was a cancellation, and the hotel books out far in advance since it's only available during winter months."

"Why would I be upset with your date? Because it falls so close to Christmas? I think it would be fun to celebrate Christmas in a wintery place like Canada. And with over a year to go, it will be easy to ensure our schedule is clear."

Ana's stomach dropped. "Uh, Papa? It isn't December of next year."

"It is not? Well then. It will be even easier to make plans for two years out. That is such a long engagement, however. Are you truly okay with that?"

She was going to throw up. "Papa, you misunderstand."

His eyebrows scrunched together. "How do I not understand? Chahna, what is going on?"

Ana licked her lips. "We're getting married this December. In two months."

The seconds ticked by as her papa stared through the camera.

"This December. I see."

She held her breath.

"That is a very...short engagement. Are we going to have a surprise in nine months?"

"Papa! No!" How could he even question that? "You know where I stand, my faith in God and His Word."

"I also know you are human."

"Yes, I am, and so is Maguire. But no. We've been very careful to set and keep our boundaries."

He nodded. "Okay. Then I will tell your mum the date and will set up the import of the tuberoses and chrysanthemums. Are there other flowers you would like?"

Her skin cooled as the embarrassment eased. Right. The flowers. What other flowers, in addition to the traditional Indian wedding flowers would she like? "What about gardenias or peonies?"

He slapped his hands together. "Consider it done."

"Thank you, Papa."

His eyes warmed. "Anything for you, Ladli."

Aw. He hadn't called her that in years.

"You're the dearest one, Papa."

"Main tumse pyar karta hoon."

"I love you, too."

They hung up just in time for Ana to run off to work. Time to focus on the Peeler account, though how she was going to do that rather than focus on her wedding, she had no clue.

By the time she arrived at work, her phone was dinging with texts from her friends. It was lunch before she could read them, and wow. Wow. She had the best friends a woman could ever hope and pray for.

LYDIA: I FOUND A DJ! ALREADY TALKED TO HIM, WHICH IS HARD WHEN I DON'T KNOW FRENCH AND HE DOESN'T HAVE ENGLISH AS HIS FIRST LANGUAGE, BUT WE DID IT. ANYWAY, I'VE BOOKED HIM AND HE'S EMAILING YOU THE CONTRACT.

CHAHNA: LYDIA! YOU'RE INCREDIBLE! THANK YOU!!!

LYDIA: GLAD YOU THINK SO. I ALSO TALKED TO NOÉMIE ABOUT YOUR CAKE, AND THE HOTEL HAS AN ON-SITE BAKER THAT SHE HIGHLY RECOMMENDS. SHE'S SENDING YOU THE INFO.

HANADY: THAT'S FANTASTIC! ANA, I PLAN ON BEING THERE. KEENAN JOKED ABOUT IT ONLY BEING ONE MORE STOP ON OUR FIRST ANNIVERSARY TRIP SINCE WE'RE HEADING TO NOLA FOR LEILAH'S WEDDING. HOW SWEET IS HE? ANYWAY, I FOUND SOME HAIRSTYLES AND WILL TOTALLY DO YOUR HAIR AND MAKEUP.

CHAHNA: YOU HAVE ME ALMOST IN TEARS.

LEILAH: NOÉMIE IS PROBABLY SICK OF HEARING FROM US. I TALKED TO HER, TOO. LOL! I'VE ARRANGED THE TRANSPORTATION FROM THE AIRPORT TO THE HOTEL.

CATE: AND I JUST HIT SEND ON YOUR INVITATIONS! ANA, THIS IS GETTING REAL!

CHAHNA: YOU GUYS. I DON'T EVEN KNOW WHAT TO SAY. THANK YOU ISN'T ENOUGH.

CATE: JUST DON'T PUT US IN HORRID BRIDESMAID DRESSES. <SHUDDER> YOU'D BE AMAZED AT WHAT'S OUT THERE THAT BRIDES CAN FIND TO TORTURE THEIR WEDDING PARTY.

CHAHNA: LOL! I PROMISE TO BE KIND. HONESTLY...BECAUSE THERE'S SO MUCH COST INVOLVED WITH THE TRAVEL, WOULD YOU BE OKAY WITH WEARING YOUR DRESSES FROM HANADY'S WEDDING? WITHOUT THE MUFFS. I'VE ALREADY CLEARED IT WITH HER. YOU'RE STILL FINE WITH IT?

HANADY: ABSOLUTELY.

CHAHNA: AND I'VE ALREADY CALLED LOVERLY! SHE WAS OVERJOYED TO SHIP A DRESS TO YOU, HAN. SHE SAID YOU WERE ONE OF THEIR FAVORITE BRIDES. ☺

HANADY: OH GOODNESS! I LOVE THOSE TWO LADIES. AND YOU, ANA! YOU BLESS ME.

Ana grinned. She was the blessed one.

CHAHNA: I NEED TO GET BACK TO WORK. LOVE YOU GUYS!

She closed the text app, slid the phone into her handbag, and got back to her desk. Her friends had taken care of most of the details. She'd be indebted for the rest of her life. And she wasn't mad about it.

There were four things in life one could be sure of: Jesus, taxes, death...and her mum's ire. Sitting on Ana's end of the phone call was uncomfortable. Thank You Lord this isn't a video call. She would hate to have to keep eye contact with her mum as she scolded her in Hindi. It was a formidable sight.

"Two months, Chahna? Two? Why can you not just wed next Christmas if this hotel means so much to you?"

"Mum." Be patient with her. "They book a year or two in advance. I wouldn't be able to get a date next year unless they had a cancellation, and even that's taking a chance. And if they did get a cancellation and they offered it to me, we'd be in this same situation."

"What is wrong with a summer wedding?" She paused. "Oh, yes. A summer wedding here in Mumbai! That would be perfect. Would you prefer May or June? Once we move into July, it's monsoon season. Even June is risky. You do not want to marry during a monsoon."

"Mum...it's hot there in the summer. And humid. I don't want my fiancé to melt." Not to mention it wasn't the ice hotel that she dreamed of.

"I just cannot have this, Chahna. Even if you do not marry in Mumbai, you absolutely cannot marry in two months. Find a different venue and change the date."

This wasn't going to end well. "No, Mum. I won't do that."

Hm. Silence really could be deafening. Who knew?

A scratching sound, like a hand covering a microphone, hinted that maybe her papa had come home and walked in on the conversation.

Muffled Hindi in a man's tone, though she couldn't make out the words, confirmed Papa was home. And the voices became louder. The last thing she wanted was to cause an argument between her parents.

"Chahna?" Her mum was back, voice tight. "Your papa and I need to discuss some things. I will call you later."

"Yes, Mum. I love you." It didn't seem that her mum had heard her, the raised voices likely drowning out her goodbye.

Ana tapped to end the call and rested the phone beside her. She needed some ibuprofen.

chapter fourteen

*I*t'd been two days since Ana last talked to her mother. In that time, her friends had completed 75% of the checklist that most brides took a year to finish. All that was left was planning the honeymoon, which really would be the few days leading up to the wedding and the week after. Mag only had ten days of leave each year, so they'd talked about staying in Québec City while their family and friends traveled back home. She'd been looking at things they could do, and called Mag with a squealing voice when she found out they could go dog-sledding.

She just didn't tell him she'd Googled about 17,000,000 photos—and saved them to her computer—of dogs pulling sleds. And looked up what it took to train for and enter the Iditarod, a new item for her Bucket List. Mag will be thrilled, she grinned.

Ana's inbox chimed with a new email. Hopefully it wasn't Jillian checking in on the Peeler account. She was making great progress, and was happy with her working relationship with Margo Peeler. Ana clicked over to her email tab.

Not from Jillian. Phew. Rather, it was from Noémie. She clicked on the subject and opened the message.

DEAR CHAHNA AND MAGUIRE,

I AM SORRY TO HEAR YOUR WEDDING HAS BEEN POSTPONED. I AM ATTACHING A CANCELLATION FORM FOR YOU TO SIGN AND RETURN AS

SOON AS POSSIBLE SINCE WE HAVE OTHER COUPLES WHO HAVE PROVISIONALLY ACCEPTED THE DATE BASED ON YOUR CANCELLATION.

IF YOU DECIDE YOU WOULD LIKE TO USE HÔTEL DE GLACE IN THE FUTURE, PLEASE REACH OUT. WE WOULD LOVE TO SERVE YOU.

REGARDS,

NOÉMIE GAGNON

Her feet felt like they swelled with all the blood in her body draining and pooling down there. What in the world? Ana sat back, breathless. What was going on here? Surely Mag hadn't cancelled their wedding. When she spoke with him that morning as she walked to work, he'd admitted he was getting excited about having their wedding in such a unique place.

She guessed the dog sledding had something to do with his change of heart.

The phone on the table beside her computer begged to be picked up so she could text him and see if he knew anything about this. But if he didn't, she didn't want to stress him out, especially while he was on duty.

No. She needed to figure this out. Ana tapped her lips with her finger. Think!

First, she needed to get a hold of Noémie. She found the number in her contacts and tapped. After speaking with reception only to find out Noémie was gone for the night, she typed out a fast email.

DEAR NOÉMIE,

I APOLOGIZE FOR ANY CONFUSION, BUT MAGUIRE AND I DO NOT WANT TO POSTPONE OUR WEDDING OR CHANGE TO A DIFFERENT VENUE. PLEASE KEEP OUR WEDDING AS SCHEDULED.

MAY I ASK WHO YOU SPOKE WITH THAT MAY HAVE GIVEN YOU THAT IDEA?

THANK YOU,

CHAHNA KAPOOR

That was done. She rubbed her upper arm. Now what? Ana choked back a sob. Don't cry. It shouldn't be too late; everything will be fine. She prayed.

While Jason was up getting a coffee refill on their break, Mag pulled his phone out of his pocket with every intention of making a quick call to Ana.

He couldn't stop the smile from spreading across his face at the thought of her. Nor did he want to.

Opening the phone, there was a new email notification. He looked up and saw Lin was talking to the guy at the counter, laughing. Knowing his partner and the barista, thanks to being regulars, Mag figured they were talking football, which meant he had a few more minutes to spare. He clicked on his email app and saw it was from Noémie.

As he read the message, his heart stuttered. What? What was this about? He looked up and stared out the window, not seeing anything but his fiancée in his mind's eye. She wouldn't have cancelled their wedding, would she? Sure, he hadn't been thrilled at the thought of getting married surrounded by ice, but the more photos he'd seen online and the more he and Ana talked about what they could do in Québec City after their wedding, the more the idea grew on him.

No, it couldn't have been her. The next thought had his heart skip a beat. The email went to both of them. Did she think he did this?

Mag fumbled his phone as he scrambled to call Ana. This wasn't me, Lass. I didn't do this.

When Ana's strained voice answered, his heart not only picked up that missed beat, but raced as if trying to beat the speed of light.

"Mag."

"It wasn't me," he choked out. Her sob resonated through the phone, replacing his blood with ice. "Please tell me you didn't think it was me."

"No," she cried with a sharp inhale. "I mean, maybe I wondered for a millisecond, but no. I knew it wasn't you."

His tensed muscles relaxed.

Ana's voice grew hesitant. "You didn't think it was me, did you?"

"Absolutely not, Lass."

She sighed. "How do you think this happened?"

"I don't know, but we need to call Noémie and make sure she doesn't officially cancel it."

"Already taken care of, babe." Ana sounded exhausted. "I tried calling, but she was gone for the day, so I sent her an email. I also asked her who gave her the idea that we wanted to cancel..."

He wondered at the trailing of her voice. "Did you think of something?"

"Mag," she whispered. "They wouldn't have, would they?"

"Who are you talking about?"

She gasped. "No. Please tell me no." He heard something scrape, as if she'd slid her chair across the floor. She must be at her little kitchen table. "Mag, I've got to go."

"Wait, what's going on?"

"My parents!" His phone chirped as the call ended.

Her parents? No way. Ana had told him her mother wasn't enthused about having a wedding so quickly, but her father had promised to import flowers, and they'd signed the wedding savings over to Ana. This couldn't have been them.

Could it?

chapter fifteen

"Papa, is Mum there with you?" Ana paced her living room, not that it offered much space. It was probably a total of ten feet in length, and maybe eight feet wide. Definitely not a lot of pacing room, especially when one was red hot angry.

"I am in the car waiting for her. We have filming today." He paused. "You do not sound good. Is everything okay?"

Ana clenched her jaw before she trusted herself enough to speak with patience. Okay. I don't trust myself to be patient. You need to give it to me, Lord. Please. "No, Papa. But I need Mum there before I talk about it."

"Well, she is coming right now."

Ana heard a door close and the murmur of her mum's voice.

"Chahna," her mother's voice sounded stressed. Because of filming, or because she just tried to ruin the happiest day of her daughter's life?

"Am I on speaker?"

"Yes," Papa said. "So, tell us what is wrong?"

"I got a message a little bit ago from the wedding coordinator at the Hôtel de Glace." She paused, wondering if they would own up to it.

Nothing.

"Someone asked her to cancel our wedding."

"What?" Papa sounded surprised.

"Oh?" Mum didn't.

She'd found the culprit. "Mum, how could you?" she wailed.

"Chahna, do not speak to your mother like that. I am sure she had nothing to do with this."

The silence said all there was needed to know.

"Shahinool, please tell me you did not do this."

"It was too short of an engagement! Chahna needed more time."

"Mum!" Tears clogged Ana's voice.

"There is no way you could have planned an entire wedding in two months. Not if it is done properly." The stubborn note to Mum's voice made Ana's teeth clench.

"My friends helped, and were finished with everything except the honeymoon and final details. When people put their heads together, a lot can be accomplished."

"But it was not done properly."

Her pent-up scream begged to be let out, and she obliged. "You don't know that! And because of that, you may have ruined my wedding!"

"Psh, don't be so dramatic, Chahna."

"Enough!" Papa's stern voice quieted both women.

"Chahna, no matter what she has done, she is still your mother. Speak to her with respect."

Ana's eyes slid shut and she swallowed her pride. "You're right, Papa." She paused. "I'm sorry for speaking to you that way, Mum."

"You are forgiven."

That was it? Ana shoved a hand through her hair, forgetting it was up in a messy bun. She untangled her fingers from the hair tie and massaged her scalp where a headache was forming.

"Shahinool." Papa again.

Her mother huffed a sigh. "You know I am right, Aariv."

There was silence, then, "Chahna, your mother and I will call you later. Please keep me," he stressed, "informed of what happens with the hotel."

A boulder so big it could probably plug up the Grand Canyon settled in her belly. "Yes, Papa."

"Main tumse pyar karta hoon."

She kept her sigh to herself because she really did love her parents. "I love you too."

After their call ended, she texted Mag.

CHAHNA: FIGURED IT OUT.

MAGUIRE: WHO?

CHAHNA: BEFORE I TELL YOU, PROMISE ME YOU'LL STILL WANT TO MARRY ME.

MAGUIRE: WHO WAS IT, ANA?

CHAHNA: PROMISE!

MAGUIRE: YOU'RE BEING DRAMATIC, YOU KNOW. ;)

She rolled her eyes. She got that dramatic gene from her mother.

MAGUIRE: OF COURSE I'LL STILL WANT TO MARRY YOU.

MAGUIRE: WAIT. DON'T TELL ME. IT WAS YOUR PARENTS, WASN'T IT?

Give the man a gold star.

CHAHNA: MORE SPECIFICALLY, MY MUM. SHE FELT TWO MONTHS WAS TOO FAST.

MAGUIRE: AH...

Ana let her head fall back so she could stare at the ceiling. The faint water stains that had been painted over a few years back were seeping through. Her phone buzzed, so she made a mental note to call her landlord and looked at the screen in her hand.

MAGUIRE: I NEED TO WRITE UP MY SHIFT REPORT. I'LL TALK TO YOU TOMORROW. I LOVE YOU.

CHAHNA: I LOVE YOU, TOO.

Mag climbed behind the wheel of his SUV and leaned his head against the headrest, scrubbing his face. It was a busy shift for him and Lin. He watched out his windshield as other officers shuffled to their cars, ready to get to bed. It was busy for everyone, judging by the quiet group.

And the night didn't end well finding out it was Shahinool who tried cancelling their wedding. Mag tapped his thumbs on the steering wheel. What made her do that? Too fast. That's what Ana had said.

Intellectually, he knew two months wasn't a long time to plan a wedding—he'd heard of some couples taking a year or more. And since his mistake of assuming he could just show up at the wedding, he'd seen Ana's friends move mountains to make this event happen.

His chest weighed down by what felt like twenty bricks, Mag turned the key in the ignition and began his trek home.

The street lights kept the city bright, but his thoughts took a dark turn. Was Shahinool right? Was it too fast? He knew marrying Ana was the right thing—she was the woman God had set aside just for him. But were they rushing the marriage just to have this wedding?

Mag pulled into his rented parking spot, gathered his equipment, and trudged up to his studio apartment. Maybe they should postpone the wedding. He didn't want to wait to marry Ana just as much as she didn't want to wait to marry him, but was that because it was right in God's eyes or because it's just what they wanted.

After he opened the door, he flicked the lights on, dropped his stuff on the kitchen table, and rummaged through his fridge looking for anything remotely healthy. A single-serving frozen lasagna wasn't so healthy, but it'd do.

As Mag waited for his dinner to heat, he pulled out his phone. Would Ana still be awake? Knowing her insomniac tendencies when she was stressed, the answer would be yes. He dialed, listening to the ringing on her end.

"Hi," she sounded breathless.

"Hey Lass. Everything okay?"

"Yeah." She huffed. "I was just jogging."

Mag glanced at the clock and his ice ran cold. "You're out running the streets at midnight?" He snatched his keys from the table. "Where are you? I'll come get you. Make sure you wait—"

"Mag, I'm not out." Her breathing had quieted.

89

"Oh. Where're you running then?"

"I'm, uh, jogging in my living room."

He knew the size of her living room. "No way."

"I am," she defended. "I'm jogging on the spot."

He barked a laugh. "Of course you are."

She groaned before speaking again. Probably sitting down. "Mag, I'm so sorry about all of this."

"Have you talked to them since?" The beeping microwave signaled his dinner was ready. He fished in the drawer for a fork and pulled the hot tray from the turntable and slid it onto a plate before taking it to the table.

"No. Papa said he'd call back but they were on their way to the studio, so I doubt I'll hear from them tonight. He wasn't happy with Mum, though."

"Really?"

"Really. Though," her voice came across sheepish, "he wasn't happy with me either."

"You?" he asked. "Why was he mad at you?"

"I lost my temper and yelled at Mum. And he's always ready to defend her to others, whether she's right or wrong, and if he feels she was in the wrong he waits to speak with her when they're alone."

Huh. That was a lesson he should take into his own marriage. "I get that."

"Yeah. I've always loved that about their marriage." She sighed. "But regardless, we are getting married in December...right?"

He took a moment to pray before answering. "Do you have any doubts about this? Do you think, even if it's the smallest doubt, that we should push pause?"

"Can we pray together and talk in the morning?"

The peace that poured over him relaxed the tension in his neck. "I think that's a perfect idea."

Together they asked the Lord to give them wisdom, to make the timing of their marriage clear to each of them, and they prayed for Ana's parents and her relationship with them through this wedding.

"Thanks, Mag." He could hear the smile in her voice.

"Love you, Lass."

"I love you too. You sound exhausted."

"Yeah," he said as he stifled a yawn. "It was a busy night. So glad tomorrow's a day off."

"I bet. You should get to bed, babe." What they said about yawns being contagious was true. Ana's yawn practically burst his ear drum.

"Okay," he laughed. "I get it. G'night."

"Goodnight."

chapter sixteen

i am sorry, Chahna." Mum turned her gaze to Mag. "And I am sorry to you, too, Maguire."

Papa cleared his throat, and Ana could've sworn she saw her mum's shoulder move. Did he just elbow her? Mum side-eyed Papa. Ha! Looks like he did.

A rush of peace passed over her when Mag, who had his arm around her shoulders, pulled her into his side. "Thank you, Shahinool," he said. "We appreciate that."

"Yes, Mum. Thank you." Okay, so what if her voice came out a little colder than she'd intended? She may have forgiven her mother, but it didn't mean she wasn't still hurt.

"Did you manage to get in touch with the hotel and save your date?" Papa leaned closer to the camera, resting his elbows on his knees.

Ana grinned at Mag. "We did." She turned back to her parents. "The coordinator there was apologetic—" she really did try to keep her voice kind— "even though it wasn't her fault."

Mum shifted, as if she were the princess sitting on the pea.

"Well," Papa clapped his hands together, "that is fantastic news. I have also ordered your flowers. They shall be flown into Québec City, then transported to the hotel two days before the wedding."

"The tuberoses, chrysanthemums, and peonies?" Ana's heart flipped. It really was coming all together.

"All of it, yes," her father smiled. "I took the liberty of adding marigolds. Those are yellow—Maguire, they symbolize brightness in our culture."

"I didn't know that. Thank you."

Ana watched Mag as he listened to her father, mirroring Papa's relaxed posture. She noticed, however, that Mum hadn't said a word throughout this call past her apology. She hadn't even looked at Ana or Mag. Was she really sorry?

"Chahna?"

"Oh, sorry, Papa. I got lost in thought."

"It's okay, Ladli." He smiled, eyes shining. "As I was saying, since the marigolds are yellow and your dresses are green—"

"Emerald, Papa. Green sounds so..." She scrunched her nose. "Not weddingish."

"I stand corrected," he grinned. "Since the dresses are emerald, and the marigolds will be a bit bright, the florist thought the peonies and chrysanthemums would be nice in jewel tones. We ordered the peonies in a dark pink, and the chrysanthemums in purple. The tuberoses will break that up nicely, according to the florist."

"That sounds gorgeous, Papa. Thank you."

"Aariv, I can't thank you enough for all you're doing. It's so generous."

"It is our pleasure, Maguire."

Ana glanced at her mum, but there was still no eye contact, no speaking. Her chest ached, but she would just have to give Mum space to work it out. She was sure to be okay by the time the wedding came around.

Right?

Maguire turned at the ding of the door. He spied Lin over the tables of ties and shirts. "Hey man," he raised his hand. Not that Jason wouldn't be able to see him. He was tall, the tables were low, and Lin wasn't short.

"Hey, groom-to-be. How ya doin'?" Jason bent at the knees then bounced forward with a jab to Mag's arm.

"Living the dream, my friend."

The salesclerk, Richard, smiled. "Do you have any other groomsmen coming today?"

"No, this guy," he wrapped the arm Jason had punched around his friend's neck in a fake chokehold, "is the only groomsman I need." That, and his other buddies were all officers, too, and had to work.

"Then let's get started."

As Richard walked them around, Jason kept picking up the ugliest ties, pocket squares, shirts, and suits.

"Man, are you truly that fashion dumb?" Mag laughed when Lin handled a white tie with green palm leaves and pink pointy flowers.

"What?" Jason held it under his chin. "I think it's great. And a wedding in an ice hotel needs some summer fun." He turned and found a mirror, studying himself with the tie.

"Well..." Richard moved toward Jason, took the tie, and laid it back down.

You're a good man, Richard.

"I think," the salesclerk said, "something different would be more appropriate for a wedding." Richard turned and faced Mag. "Did I hear something about an ice hotel?"

"Yep," he grinned. "Up in Canada."

Richard nodded. "That's awesome. Let me show you what I'm thinking."

Forty-five minutes and one palm leaf tie later, Mag and Jason left with receipts to pick up their tuxedos three days before they flew out.

"Thanks for coming, Lin. I appreciate it." The midday sun was warm on Mag's skin. He might need to see if he could talk Ana into going out on some kayaks later.

"Wouldn't miss it for the world. Hey," Jason motioned with his chin toward a coffee shop.

"Sounds good."

Once Mag had his dirty chai and Jason his black coffee, they sat in a couple of club chairs.

"Have things settled with Ana's mom?"

Mag sipped his drink before setting it on the coffee table between them. "I really don't know. We talked with her parents yesterday and her mam apologized, but she didn't say anything after that. I guess we'll see."

Lin nodded but didn't say anything. He was fine at the tux shop but now looked distracted.

"You okay?"

"What? Oh. Yeah, I'm good." He ducked his head. "Really good."

"I like hearing that. What's up?"

"Maya's pregnant."

His friend said it so simply, but it was big news. Huge. "What? Congratulations, man!"

"Thanks," Jason grinned.

"When did you find out? And why didn't you say something earlier?"

"Yesterday, and because we had to get you a tux. I personally look sharp in anything, but you? You need all the help you can get."

Mag barked a laugh. "Seriously, I'm happy for you. How did you find out? I thought the in vitro didn't work."

"The last round didn't. Without getting into the details—"

"Thanks for that," Mag laughed.

Jason lowered his chin with a regal air. "You're quite welcome." He smiled. "Maya was having some symptoms a couple of weeks after retrieval, so they did an exam yesterday. And there you have it." Lin sat straight in his chair, deepened his voice, and said loud enough for those around them to hear, "I have spawned!"

The guy had problems...but humor wasn't one of them.

"So now Maya and I really need to move."

"Well, Ana and I are on to help tomorrow."

"Thanks. Now about that mother-in-law of yours, I have some words of wisdom to pass on."

Of course he did. Mag rolled his eyes, but sat forward and listened anyway. Shahinool really was a sweet woman and he was sure it'd all work out, but it didn't hurt to learn from another person's experience.

chapter seventeen

December 21st

Snow glittered like diamonds as the plane descended into Québec City. Little diamonds of death. Those slippery flakes could kill them before their jet came to a taxiing speed on the runway.

"Lass, you're breaking my fingers."

Ana shuddered, and it had nothing to do with Mag's rich, smooth voice. "Did I ever tell you I don't like flying?"

Mag looked down at his purple fingers where she'd cut off his circulation. "I would've never guessed," he said dryly.

The brakes squealed as the plane bounced on touchdown. She really, really wished teleportation was a thing. But God, gravity, and brakes soon had the plane slowed and taxiing to their gate.

Thank You, Lord.

The Jean Lesage International Airport welcomed them with large floor-to-ceiling windows and modern furniture decorated with garland and varying styles of Christmas trees throughout. It was bright and open, but after a red eye flight, all Ana wanted for Christmas was a hot coffee and comfy bed.

Bed. There was something about beds she wanted to—

OH NO. Ana clapped a hand over her mouth. In her excitement for the hotel, she'd kept a key detail to herself when describing it to Mag. The beds. Best to wait until they were in their rental car before telling him. And maybe he'd looked at the photos closely and seen the beds and didn't care. One could hope.

Mag led them through the outskirts of the city and soon they were on a highway surrounded by trees on both sides.

It was now or never.

"So, babe."

"Hm?"

"About the hotel..."

He glanced at her before looking down at the Google Map and back up to the highway. "What's up?"

"Well the beds there are, well...made of ice."

Mag's eyes squinted. It was kind of bright out there, with snow off to the sides of the road. "What's that again?"

"The beds—"

"I heard what you said, Ana. But what does that mean?"

She knew he wasn't dumb, not even close. But really? She wrinkled her nose. "What do you mean, 'what does that mean'?"

"I mean, the beds are made of ice. But surely you don't sleep straight on the ice."

"Well, no. I saw a Hallmark movie filmed there, and they had sleeping bags." She tried her best to give him the brightest smile. No need to scare the man off.

"Sleeping bags," he repeated in a monotone.

This wasn't going well, but at least he hadn't turned the car around to go back to the airport.

Baby steps.

"I guess we'll see when we get there." The long inhale that accompanied those words gave her pause.

Maybe he'd turn the car around after all.

"Bienvenue, Monsieur Wilson et Mademoiselle Kapoor. We are happy to have you at Hôtel de Glace. Did you have a lovely trip?"

Mag's hand still didn't have all the blood back from Ana's squeezing it, but it was still a good trip. "We did, thanks."

"And you, mademoiselle? How are you feeling about sleeping here tonight?" Edouard—Mag read the check-in guy's poinsettia nametag—asked.

Ana's eyes grew three sizes bigger. "Wh-why would I be feeling anything other than excited?"

Yeah. He wanted the answer to her question, too.

Edouard waved his hand in front of his face. "No matter. Now," he rubbed his hands together, "there are a few things for you to do before you take possession of your room. First, there is a required briefing. In this, you'll learn about how to sleep, dress, and what to do in your room. Second, all rooms are open to the public for touring until eight o'clock at night. At that time, staff will close the rooms off to non-guests and prepare your room for you. You may take possession at nine o'clock."

Mag could admit he didn't really do any homework about the hotel—he'd left that all up to Ana. And he was beginning to question his judgment.

"If, at any time during the night, you feel you cannot stand it—and please know, it isn't from the cold, most people get too hot in their sleeping bags—every booking of an ice room comes with a room at the main hotel. You may move to that room if you grow uncomfortable."

His summer-loving heart suddenly felt much lighter. "Well that's a relief."

Ana smacked his arm. "Come on. You don't think you can tough it out?"

"Since we aren't staying in the same room for these first two nights," he watched as a fire lit her eyes, "I guess you'll never know." He wagged his eyebrows for good measure.

Rolling her eyes, Ana turned back to Edouard. "Are we able to take possession of our normal rooms right now?"

"Oui, of course." Edouard passed their room cards to them and showed them where the briefing would be.

"I wonder if my parents are here yet?" Ana craned her neck, looking around.

"I'm sure we'll know soon enough. Your parents kind of stand out."

"What do you mean?" Ana's eyes narrowed.

"Chahna!" Her mother's voice carried across the open area, garnering several looks. Mag just lifted one brow and grinned at Ana who rolled her eyes and turned toward her mam.

"Mum, hi!" They leaned in for a hug. "When did you and Papa get here? Where is he?"

"He is on his way down. He just had a phone call to make."

"Lass." He waited until Ana looked at him. "While you two get caught up, I'm going to check out the hotel. Is that okay?"

She reached up and kissed him. "Of course."

With a wave, Mag walked across the snowy ground toward the arched wooden doors that stood open to the Hôtel de Glace, his exhales creating clouds so cold they were almost opaque.

As he stepped through the doors, his jaw dropped. No way. Not only did they have electricity inside, they'd placed colored lights behind thick walls of ice that intensified the blue hue around the room. His eyes followed the carvings and sculptures up to the ceiling where a chandelier made of ice—no way!—hung, again with a light fixed in the center. A large Christmas tree carved out of ice with colored lights frozen inside—how did they do that?—stood in the center of the lobby.

Okay, he was starting to get what made Ana book this place.

Mag followed some people down a hall—again with shapes and pictures carved into them—toward the guest suites. He stuck his head into a room with a blue curtain. It was small and simple, nothing special about it. Except, you know, the fact it was solid ice and snow, and had a Christmas wreath hanging above the bed.

The next room had a red curtain. Mag stepped through it and, manly man that he was, he gasped. Get out. The room had a queen-sized bed on a platform of ice. Across from the bed stood a fireplace—he reached out to feel the heat, but there was none. Must be decoration only. But while those two things alone were incredible, it wasn't what made him gasp. Above the bed was an arched shape, and in that shape, an artist painted the ice in an almost abstract manner. It was clear, though, the varying blues that met varying greens halfway down the arch were sky and grass. And in the grass were painted red roses. Surrounding the bed on the walls and at the foot were more painted grass and roses. Garland framed the room like crown moulding. He pushed his hand on the mattress and raised his eyes to heaven, thanking the Lord. It was a thick, soft mattress. Mag looked around and, not seeing anyone, lifted the corner of the mattress. A sheet of plywood separated the mattress from the ice.

He had to get Ana. She'd die. But first, he wanted to explore more.

Stepping out of the room, he looked in a few more rooms, each as crazy-awesome as the others, then followed a map on the wall to the bar. As he walked, he passed by a set of stairs carved into the snow with ice handrails. There was nothing else to say but it was beautiful. And a good place to take a wedding photo, he mentally noted. He watched as people—kids and adults—climbed the stairs. On the other side, some of those same people appeared, laughing. Mag jog-walked over there only to discover it was a slide. A slide!

No way was he passing this up!

He followed two kids up the stairs and waited until it was his turn. He sat at the top of the slide, thankful he'd worn his winter gear, and pushed off.

Sliding down ice was the coolest—every pun intended—thing ever! He couldn't help the laugh that escaped as he went around a bend and came to the end. He jumped up, brushing his rear-end off.

"Have fun?" The laughter in Ana's voice greeted him. As did the smirks of her parents.

Whatever. He grinned. What happened at the ice hotel stayed at the ice hotel. Or something like that. "A ton. You want to try?"

"I don't know," Ana said.

Oh, what an opening she just left him. "Why not? Cold feet?"

Aariv barked a laugh while Ana just groaned. Shahinool covered her eyes, but her shoulders shook.

This was going to be a fun week.

chapter eighteen

*A*na shook her hands out and bounced on her feet.

"Relax, girl," Hanady grabbed her hand. "This is just the rehearsal."

"I know. I don't know why I'm so nervous about this."

Cate came up behind her and wrapped her arms around Ana's shoulders and squeezed. "Han's right. Don't worry about it. And besides," she let go and walked around to Ana's front, eyeing her. "You look incredible."

Ana looked down at her outfit. Normally this would be what an Indian woman would wear to her actual wedding, but since she had a traditional wedding gown for that, her parents had this made as a surprise for her to wear to the rehearsal and following dinner.

Her heart skipped a beat as she took in the gold embroidery of the long rose-red skirt. The short matching choili, basically a capped sleeve crop top, hugged her rib cage. Normally she wouldn't wear something that exposed her stomach like this, but it was tradition, and she couldn't help herself. The dupatta had matching embroidery—heavy around the scalloped edges like her skirt—and laid over the top of her head, flowing down to just below her knees, like a western veil. The wedding lehenga—the whole outfit—was stunning.

Ana's arms tinkled with the sounds of the abundance of gold bangles wrapped around her wrists as she reached up to adjust the Maang Tikka, the small piece of jewelry centered on her forehead. It matched the gold and diamond earrings and necklace she wore.

"I can't believe how much jewelry you're wearing," Cate said. "It's incredible."

"Probably too much." Ana eyed the rings on her fingers.

"No," her friend protested. "It's gorgeous. I don't think it would look right if you didn't have it all."

"Chahna." Mum walked into the room, Papa trailing behind, only to stop in her tracks. "Oh, Chahna."

Papa's eyes welled. He strode forward and picked up her hands in his. "Ladli, you look beautiful." He leaned forward and kissed her cheek.

"Thank you, Papa." Ana looked over his shoulder. "And Mum...thank you so much for everything. The flowers, this lehenga, the jewelry. It's so generous."

Mum worked her jaw before answering. "It is the least I could do after I hurt you and Maguire." She stepped toward Ana, who reached out and hugged her. "I am so sorry."

"All is forgiven, Mum." Ana leaned back to look at her. "Honest."

Her mum's lips pressed together and she nodded, her own eyes bright with unshed tears.

"Well," Papa said. "I believe it is time for this rehearsal."

Hanady grinned. "Let's go!"

Man, was he ever happy the rehearsal was in the regular hotel rather than the one made of ice. He'd hate to be standing at the end of the aisle in his kilt turning blue and likely getting hypothermic. Mag looked out one of the room's windows. Yeah. Definitely cold out there. Snow was falling onto the already snowy resort. The beige and wood interior of this function room was made even more warm and welcoming because of the weather outside. The Christmas tree in the corner lit with white lights and garland framing the windows also helped.

"Maguire," Noémie called from the door to the room, "Ana is ready. We may begin, Monsieur Côté."

Beside Maguire, the officiant looked up from his notes. "Bien."

Noémie nodded and backed out of the door, closing it behind her. A man in a sound booth in the back corner of the room must have flipped a switch because Storybook Love's opening notes flowed through the overhead speakers. Mag grinned, happy Ana had let him choose the Princess Bride song for the processional.

The doors opened. First Hanady walked through, followed by Lydia, Leilah—

Whoa! Leilah was walking! Mag's arms pebbled. When did that happen? How? Did Ana know about this? He shook his head. Ana must know about it since she was standing around the corner.

Cate rounded through the door and Mag's heart skipped. Ana was next. All her friends watched him—he could feel their stares, but he kept his eyes glued to the doors as they closed behind Cate.

When the music had its little crescendo moment, the doors opened and Mag's lungs stopped working. Ana rounded the corner in her full, traditional Indian wedding outfit.

She literally stole his breath.

Ana's heart stuttered and her mouth dried as she spied her fiancé.

Mag stood tall, almost a head above their officiant. Her gaze started at his feet where he wore black Oxford dress shoes topped with black knee-length socks. And...he was wearing his kilt! She'd begged him to, but the little brat gave her a resounding no every time she brought it up. His Wilson clan tartan, with its red background and blue, green, and white stripes, hugged his hips and ended right above his socks. He kept his outfit casual, however, with a white button-down dress shirt, the sleeves rolled up to his elbows. Around his wrist he wore two wood bead bracelets and two chunky silver chain bracelets.

But it was his glowing hazel eyes that grabbed and held her attention.

One more day. Just one, and he'll be mine forever.

chapter nineteen

A rap at the door woke Ana. She opened her eyes to bright light streaming in through the crack between the two curtains covering the window.

This is our wedding day! Ana whipped back the comforter and called, "Hold on! I'm coming." The sheets had a different idea, though. She didn't realize her feet were tangled and as she tried to jump out of the bed, they held her ankles and she fell forward.

"Gah!"

Another knock and she heard Lydia's voice. "Ana? Are you okay? We heard a...scream?"

"I'm fine," Ana called.

She took stock of her situation. The blood rushed to her head as she bent over the edge of the bed, her feet still tangled in the sheets, her hands braced on the floor.

The giggles turned to a full-on belly laugh. This wasn't how she pictured starting her wedding day.

"Give me a second." Her voice strained as she yelled out. Ana crawled her hands along the floor while she kicked and twisted her feet to free herself from the sheet. Finally extricating herself, she stood, pulled her wide-leg pajama bottoms up and her t-shirt down, and opened the door to Lydia, Hanady, Leilah, and Cate.

"I miss Ruthie," she said.

The girls all nodded with Lydia voicing her feelings. "Me too."

"But," said Cate, "she's FaceTiming in, so while she isn't here in person, she still won't miss it."

Ana shrugged. "Still not as good as having her here."

"I know." Hanady reached over and hugged her.

"Well, get on in here." Ana stood away from the door and let the girls, all carrying their dress bags, into her suite.

"That dress," breathed Leilah. "I can't wait to see you in it."

Ana studied the gown hanging from the French door leading to the bedroom. The trumpet-style dress was simple, with just the right amount of lace and beading. Her heart worked overtime at the thought of putting it on.

"Let's get to work, girls!" Hanady clapped her hands together once. "Ana, get your shower and dry your hair, but don't put anything in it. I'll take care of that."

"Thanks, Han." Ana hugged her friend.

"Anything for you. Just don't take long."

Ana raced through the shower, which was no small feat considering the amount of hair she had, and had her teeth brushed, mouthwash done, and plenty of deodorant on before she donned her undergarments for the dress and the white robe with Bride written in rhinestones on the back. A little garish, but come on. It was her wedding day!

The girls spent the next couple of hours getting themselves ready, then Hanady focused all her attention on Ana, doing first her hair, then her makeup.

"So, your hair. I was thinking of doing some loose curls and pulling most of it back into a very loose, low ponytail and leaving a few tendrils to frame your face. I think that would suit you perfectly. What do you think?"

Ana's mind raced too fast to picture it. "Honestly, whatever you think will work, I'll be happy with." She bounced her knee.

Across the room, Cate laughed. "A little excited there, Ana?"

"Huh? What gave you that idea?" She giggled. "Just a little."

The door to the suite clicked and her mum poked her head in. "Hello ladies." She walked in, letting the door swing shut behind her and eyed Ana's friends. "You all look lovely."

A knock made her mum turn and open the door back up. "Oh, the flowers. Thank you."

A woman Ana didn't recognize carried in a box. "Noémie asked me to deliver the bouquets to you," she said as she placed the box on a table then turned toward Ana. "The chapel is ready, and the boutonnieres are with the men."

"Thank you," Ana called as the woman left. She eyed her mum out of the corner of her eye. "Mum, you look beautiful."

Mum wore a deep red saree with delicate gota patti embroidery. She kept her jewelry simple with gold and diamond stud earrings and bangles.

"Thank you, Chahna," she smiled as she picked her phone out of her clutch and glanced at the screen. "I do believe it is time for you to dress."

Ana's stomach fluttered. "It...it is?" Hoo, she needed some water.

As if she'd been reading Ana's mind, Lydia appeared with a glass of cool water and handed it to her.

"Thanks, Lyd."

Her friend smiled and stepped back. Cate stood on a step stool and reached up to pull the wedding gown off the door.

Ana blew a breath out. "Okay, let's do this."

The girls held the dress over Ana's head and lowered it, hands first, until the waist of the gown settled. Leilah and Cate helped Ana as she slid her arms through the sheer cap sleeves, and her mum zipped the gown until it ended just above her waist. The back of the dress was one of her favorite parts. The deep v of the gown exposed most of her back until it pointed in near her waist.

Leilah, in her wheelchair so she wouldn't be too exhausted to walk down the aisle, held a box in her lap that set Ana's heart quivering.

The tiara.

Her friend grinned up at her, blinking back tears. "Are you ready?"

Grabbing her lips between her teeth, Ana nodded. Leilah opened the box and carefully removed the snowflake tiara, passing it first to Hanady, then to Lydia, who took a moment to study the headpiece Ana knew she thought she'd never wear, and finally to Cate.

Her best-of-best friend reached up and, with Hanady's help, secured the tiara to Ana's head. All the girls and her mum stepped back.

Complete silence.

Uh-oh. Did it look terrible? Was something wrong with her dress? Her makeup?

Ana looked down at herself. Nothing seemed out of place, but— She glanced back up at the women in front of her. "Is everything okay?"

Her mum rubbed her hands under her eyes. "It is more than okay. You are the most beautiful bride I have ever seen, Ladli."

Ana could swear she was floating on air. "Thank you, Mum." Now to go meet the answer to her prayers at the altar.

"You ready?" Jason stood in front of Mag, his bright smile spreading his face.

"Very. Do I look okay?" Mag turned to face the full-length mirror in his room. The black tux was traditional, but the pocket square... He smoothed the silk brocade made up of all the colors of the flowers in their wedding. Aariv had gifted it to him earlier when he stopped by to welcome Mag to the family.

"Yeah, you're fine." His partner smirked then shook his head. "I still can't believe you had boxers made out of your clan tartan."

"Hey, it's a nod to my heritage, just like this," he pointed to the pocket, "is a nod to Ana's."

Jason opened his mouth, but a knock on the door interrupted whatever he was going to say. Instead, he moved to open the door. "Hi. Can I help you?"

Mag didn't hear what was said, focusing instead on adjusting his tie. He spied movement in the mirror over his shoulder. When he looked more closely, eyes the color of his smiled at him. He jerked around, a flash of adrenaline spiking his pulse.

"Mam!" He rushed to her and swooped her small frame into his arms. Her tinkling laugh soothed all his nerves and he set her back down. "What are you doing here? I thought you couldn't come."

Her gentle Scottish brogue was music to his ears. "A mam does what she has to in order to be at her only child's wedding."

His mam may be small, but she was the most determined woman he'd ever met aside from Ana. He'd been sad when she said she couldn't get off work. Being married straight out of school, she hadn't had an easy go of it after his father left, working one, sometimes two, jobs to keep their little family afloat. Which begged the question...

"How did you afford the flight? I'll send you money to cover the ticket."

She shook her head. "No, but thank you. It's been taken care of."

The only people he knew who could afford a last-minute plane ticket were Ana's parents. He'd thank them in private later. Mam was a proud woman, so accepting their help must have been hard, and he wouldn't bug her about it and make her uncomfortable.

"I'm so happy you're here, Mam." He looked down at her simple dress. The burgundy velvet suited her silver hair and hazel eyes. "You look beautiful."

A blush pinked her cheeks. "Thank you."

Jason appeared behind his mam. "I hate to break this up but," he tapped the watch on his wrist, "it's time to go."

Time to go. Time to get married.

chapter twenty

Standing at the end of the aisle, this time in the Hôtel de Glace chapel, was...well, Mag didn't know how to describe the feeling. He stared at the arched wooden double doors at the other end, past the twenty guests who sat two-by-two on ice-sculpted benches covered with furs. Beside the bench ends sat lanterns with flickering candles inside, each lantern topped with a spray of the flowers Aariv had ordered and flown in. The marigolds, chrysanthemums, peonies, and tuberoses also circled the ice pillars on either side of him.

Mag's ears were probably frozen, but his nerves had his blood running hot. He rubbed his black-gloved hands together and bounced on his toes.

"Take it easy, Romeo."

Mag side-eyed Jason. "Who made you best man, anyway?"

His partner grinned. Just in the nick of time, the music played at the rehearsal strained through speakers.

Like déjà vu, the double doors opened and Hanady walked through, carrying her bouquet with white-gloved hands. Next came Lydia, then Leilah—gingerly measuring each step down the snowy aisle—and finally Cate, Ana's maid of honor. Mag squinted at Cate's bouquet. Was that...was that a phone nestled in it?

He hid his laugh behind a hand. He could almost guarantee there was a very pregnant Ruth Ann getting a front row seat to the action. When he met Cate's gaze, she flicked her gaze at the phone then winked at him.

Yep. Definitely Ruth Ann.

Once Cate took her place, she turned and whispered to Leilah, who smiled and mouthed, I'm okay to her.

He couldn't wait to get to know this special group of women—and their husbands and boyfriends—better.

Mag turned his gaze back to the doors that had closed behind Cate and waited, his heart palpitating. This was it.

The doors opened and Aariv stepped forward wearing what Ana had told him was called a sherwani. The ivory-colored buttoned-up jacket hung below Aariv's knees, covering most of the same-colored pants. He wore a pocket square that matched the ones Mag and Jason wore.

But on his arm was the most precious jewel. Ana stepped forward in her white gown. Most of the dress looked plain, hugging her hips then gently flaring out above her knees.

His mouth dried.

She wore a faux fur wrap and white gloves to keep her warm. There was no veil, but on her head sat a sparkling crown of some sort. As she drew closer, it came into focus. Was that a snowflake? It looked like one. Mag grinned.

He'd once read that no one snowflake was like any other. That described his bride perfectly.

The reception back in the main hotel was lively and everything Ana had hoped for. They didn't have many guests, but those who were there laughed, danced under the white twinkle lights and mistletoe, and mingled like nobody's business. She would have loved for the reception to be in the ice bar, but didn't even bother to ask Noémie if that was possible after seeing the tense jaw of her now-husband.

Husband. Maguire Wilson was now hers forever. She was Chahna Tanvi Wilson. Thank You, Lord.

"Hey Ana," Cate appeared beside her. "How are you feeling, Mrs. Wilson?"

Ana tilted her head back, smiling at the ceiling. She'd never tire of hearing that name.

"Did I hear my name?" Mag's mum turned then saw Ana. "Oh dear, I'm sorry. You are," she grinned, "the new Mrs. Wilson." Lynda reached out and hugged her. "I am so happy for you and my son."

"Thank you, Lynda. I'm honored to be part of your family."

"The honor is ours, dear. I've never seen Maguire happier." She hugged Ana once more then stepped back. "Speaking of," Lynda cocked her head to the side and looked past Ana's shoulder.

When she turned, Ana saw her husband standing there. His eyes sparkled with life and joy and love.

"Are you ready to blow this joint, Lass?" He wagged his eyebrows, causing heat to flame her cheeks. He'd pay for that.

Ana let her gaze roam his body, pausing on his lips before ending at his eyes. Ha! Her husband's face burned brighter than the fire in the fireplace at the other end of the room.

Paid in full.

"More than ready, Jaanu."

Mag's brows scrunched together. "What does Jaanu mean?"

She grinned. "Do your homework," she said as she brushed by him, waving at Jason whose shoulders bounced with laughter. "I'm ready for our night in the ice hotel." Behind her, Mag groaned.

"I mean, those rooms are amazing, but do you really want to sleep there?"

She tossed what she hoped was a sassy grin over her shoulder but didn't say anything, and walked out of the room, their guests none the wiser. They'd already done a sparkler arch as she and Mag left the chapel walking under it. No need for them to break up the party just to watch them walk across some snow into the Hôtel de Glace.

When she and Mag stepped outside, they jolted to a stop. Above the flowing hotel, the sky lit up with varying shades of green. The aurora borealis! She hadn't even dreamed of the possibility of seeing them. The thought hadn't even crossed her mind. But there she stood, beside the husband of her prayers, after her dream wedding, dazed by the sight. The few guests outside at this time of night also stood still, watching the incredible sight.

Mag wrapped an arm around her shoulders and pulled her close, resting his cheek against her temple. Hot breath fanned her ear as he whispered, "I love you, Lass."

She turned her head, her body tingling from head to toe and her heart fluttering. "I love you too, Jaanu."

He shook his head. "You really need to tell me—"

Several weeks ago, she'd learned what it was like being quieted with a kiss. Now it was his turn. Ana wrapped her arms around her husband, leaned into him and brushed her lips across his. The gentle touch fanned the sparks to roaring flames as Mag responded, deepening the kiss, his arms drawing her closer.

After what felt like the best forever, she leaned back, panting for breath. "You...are the...best Christmas gift ever." She moved in for another kiss.

"And you, Lass. You are better than any gift of any kind ever received."

"I can't believe I get to spend this Christmas with you as my husband."

"Merry Christmas, Lass."

"Merry Christmas, Jaanu."

Mag covered her mouth with his lips, making her happier than Santa ever had.

epilogue

hey'd actually made it through the night. Ana woke beside her husband, shifted her arms outside the sleeping bag and stretched. Down the hall came the forewarned wake-up call. Mag stirred and grumbled, one arm resting across his eyes.

"It's too early," he rasped.

She laughed. Her husband definitely wasn't a morning person. "No, it's 8:30. We have a half-hour to get out of bed, get dressed, and check out of this room. We can go back to bed when we get to our hotel room."

Mag turned his head, his ginger hair mussed up. It did a number on her stomach. "That sounds good."

A few hours later, they walked into the hotel restaurant, ready for some brunch.

Mum and Papa sat beside Lynda, chattering away. It was so good to see the three of them getting along. Jason and Maya—she couldn't get over the fact they were pregnant—were talking with Cate, Leilah, Leilah's husband, Reggie, Lydia, and Hanady and Keenan. She and Mag sat in the seats beside Mag's partner and his wife, across from Leilah and Reggie.

"How are the newlyweds?" Leilah's smile widened her face.

"You tell me," Ana laughed.

Her friend pointed at Ana. "Good point."

The group talked for the next hour, enjoying their meals. Ana watched as Cate excused herself to go to the restroom. She had a sudden need to go herself. She snatched her tote and followed her friend.

"Hey Cate, I'm following."

Cate turned and smiled. "I think the myth is true about women never going to the bathroom alone."

Ana laughed. "It's at least true in our group's case." She glanced back at the table where the rest of their friends still sat talking. "Well...maybe just in our—" she pointed between herself and Cate— "case."

When they finished in the bathroom, they rambled back. Ana stopped her best friend with her hand. "Cate."

Cate turned soulful eyes on her. "What's up?"

Ana rummaged in her tote, found what she was looking for, and held out the box. "I do believe this now belongs to you." In her outstretched hand she held the glittering snowflake tiara that had been passed down from Ruthie to Leilah, then to Ana, and now give to Cate. "You're next," she said with a wink.

Cate stared at the crown, a smile playing across her lips. She reached out and touched it. "Are you sure you're ready to part with it already?"

"For my best friend? I sure am."

Cate wrapped her fingers around the tiara and with her other arm hugged Ana. "Thank you." She straightened and put the tiara back in Ana's hand. "But can you keep it until I actually need it? I'm afraid it'll get lost before I can ever get married."

"It'll happen, prayerfully sooner than you think. I can't wait for your wedding day." Ana's eyes teared up at the thought of her sweet friend finally marrying the man of her own dreams.

They walked arm-in-arm back to their table, Ana whispering a prayer that by this time next year, her friend would have her own happily ever after.

author's note

*i*n my research, I learned that the Hôtel de Glace isn't actually open when this tale takes place. I decided to run with it anyway and took some "artistic license" to have it open. I hope you'll forgive me, but it was too unique a location for a winter wedding to pass up.

The Hôtel de Glace officially opened in 2001 and opens each year from January to March. And seriously, you should check out the photos! Each year, they have a different theme for the hotel, and each room has its own unique design. It's an incredible venue (Hallmark filmed Winter Castle there if you'd like to see it "in real life") full of romance and magic. I highly recommend you find a photo (or 17,000,000 like Chahna—and I—did) and dream up your own stories.

Mike

PS – I just found out that Google Maps Street View has interior shots of the hotel! So you can get up close and personal all from the warmth of your own home. I love technology.

acknowledgements

First, as always, I want to thank my Lord and Saviour, Jesus. Without Him, this whole writing thing wouldn't happen—not only would He not have blessed me with this gift, but I would have given up long ago. Writing is no joke!

I also want to thank my sweet friends, Toni, Jaycee, Teresa, and Andrea. Thank you for letting me come back to this collection group for a second time! I don't know what you were thinking...

Angela Ruth Strong, we missed you in this story! But were happy to have Ruth Ann. <3 Maybe you'll be able to join us again in the future and make this author group complete.

Lyndsey, thank you sooooo much for praying for me, for encouraging me...and for nagging me. Everyone needs a friend exactly like you in their lives. You're a gift.

Jaycee and Teresa, another shout out! Thank you for saving my sanity!! This story really didn't feel like it was coming together AT ALL until you read it, made some suggestions and gave me ideas, and just loved on me.

E.V.E. (my kids), I love you. Thank you for your patience as I sat at my computer for hours on end, especially toward the end. Thank you for the sneak-attack hugs. Thank you for the phone calls. You all make me so incredibly proud, for your love for God, your love for others, your love for me, and your love for one another.

Mark, you're my heart outside my body. I love you. (And thank you for making dinner...a lot. And doing the laundry. And installing the new microwave.)

I started writing this story at the beginning of 2020 with every intention of having it finished by late spring. Turns out that 2020 laughed at my plans. Not only is there a global pandemic outside my window, but there were some hard, grievous times for my family, my friends, and my coworkers. It was hard to think lighthearted enough to write this story amid dark moments, but my friends...those dark moments just made our God's light that much brighter.

> "But God, who is rich in mercy, because of his great love that he had for us, made us alive with Christ even though we were dead in trespasses. You are saved by grace! He also raised us up with him and seated us with him in the heavens in Christ Jesus, so that in the coming ages he might display the immeasurable riches of his grace through his kindness to us in Christ Jesus. For you are saved by grace through faith, and this is not from yourselves; it is God's gift—not from works so that no one can boast. For we are his workmanship, created in Christ Jesus for good works, which God prepared ahead of time for us to do" (Ephesians 2:4-10, CSB).

about the author

Mikal Dawn is an inspirational romance author, wedding enthusiast, and proud military (retired) wife. By day, she works as an administrative assistant for an international ministry organization, runs her kids to all their sports, and drinks lots of coffee. By night, she pulls her hair out, wrestling with characters and muttering under her breath as she attempts to write while dinner is burning. And drinks lots of coffee. When she isn't writing about faith, fun, and forever, she is obsessively scouring Pinterest (with coffee in hand, of course!) for wedding ideas for her characters.

Originally from Vancouver, Canada, Mikal now lives in Oklahoma with her husband, Mark, two of their three children, and one lazy, ferocious feline who can often be found taking over her Instagram account. Find Mikal on mikaldawn.com, Facebook, Twitter, Instagram, Goodreads, Bookbub, and Pinterest.

more books by mikal dawn

Emerald City Romance Series
Count Me In
If She Dares: A Novella
Claim My Heart : A Novella
(found in the Once Upon a Christmas collection)

A Holly, Bolly Christmas: A Novella